Live the Dream . . .

This is the unforgettable story of Maggie Callahan's struggle to survive in the wilderness of Central Pennsylvania.

Here is a chance to step back 200 years, into an era filled with danger and mystery and incredible beauty.

Maggie's tale is a rich blend of heart-pounding adventure, interpretive history and good, old-fashioned storytelling, created especially for children and dreamers of all ages.

The Bread Sister of Sinking Creek

LIFE ON THE PENNSYLVANIA FRONTIER

by Robin Moore

illustrated by William Sauts Bock

published by Groundhog Press
P.O. Box 93, Wyncote, PA 19095

LIBRARY OF CONGRESS CATALOGUE NO. 84-60397

ISBN 0-9613433-1-1 (Paperback)
ISBN 0-9613433-2-X (Hardback)

FIRST PRINTING: WINTER 1984
SECOND PRINTING: SPRING 1985

This book is dedicated to three strong women:

My mother, Jeanne Catherine Moore
Who filled my boyhood days with the smells of fresh-baked bread.

My wife, Jacque Sonstein Moore
Who believed in Maggie's story from the start and kept the flame alive.

To my daughter, Rachel Sonstein Moore
Who was born along with this book and has it all ahead of her . . .

Contents

About The Story

I first dreamed up the story of The Bread Sister in the winter of 1975, while I was living in an old wooden cabin up on the mountainside above Sinking Creek, in the Seven Mountains region of Central Pennsylvania.

Maggie's story grew like tall corn in July. But I wasn't interested in writing it down. I was too busy splitting firewood and weeding the garden and baking bread to worry about making a book.

When I left the cabin for a new life of writing and storytelling in Philadelphia, I carried Maggie's story along with me. But I was too busy fighting for economic survival to take on a risky and hopelessly romantic project like writing a book.

Finally, the time was right. Seven years after I first

discovered her, I sat and wrote down Maggie's story, making it into a book that folks could read and enjoy. After carrying the story in my head all those years, it was almost like writing down a dream remembered from another time.

The story of The Bread Sister takes place in the Central Pennsylvania wilderness in the 1770's. While Maggie is a fictional character, General Potter, Joseph McGrew and many of the other characters which appear here are not. I've done my best to make the historical details as accurate as possible, combining library research with my own first-hand experiences of living up on the mountainside in the old-time way. I believe this approach gives a credible view of what life might have been like for a girl like Maggie Callahan.

I am indebted to Donna Munger, of The Pennsylvania Historical and Museum Commission, who carefully read the manuscript and made several suggestions which improved the story while maintaining historical accuracy. I thank her for sharing her knowledge with me.

While I am being thankful, I should say a word about the illustrator, William Sauts Bock. Working with him has been a joy. He knows how to draw the dream. His magnificent illustrations really make Maggie come alive. I thank him for his contribution to this book.

Judy Foulke and Betty Schoen offered invaluable help in putting this book together. They read the manuscript and gave insightful comments as well as handling the editing and proofreading. I thank them.

By the way, this book is designed to be read aloud, in the old-fashioned tradition of family evenings by the fireside. Each chapter is about a night's worth of reading. You might want to do it that way. Enjoy the story. Live the dream.

Robin Moore
Summer 1984

Chapter One

It was a hot afternoon, late in the summer of 1776, deep in the heart of the Pennsylvania wilderness. A hunched-over old man and a red-haired girl came riding single-file up the mountain trail with a string of packhorses roped between them.

At the head of the packstring rode Herbert Johnson, a mountain tinker who traveled from one wilderness community to another, peddling the trade goods carried on the backs of his pack animals.

He was a gnarled, hunched-over old man, old and worn down like the mountains he rode through. Despite the heat, he wore a long overcoat, blackened and grease-stained from a thousand campfires.

His eyes were small and close together, like a possum's,

and they peered out from under the wide brim of his hat, searching the trail ahead. His chin-whiskers pointed the way up the mountainside.

Stepping along behind Mr. Johnson were his pack-horses, heavily loaded now and roped together so they'd stay to the trail.

At the end of the packstring rode Maggie Callahan.

She was fourteen years old that summer. She was a fine-looking girl, with a touch of the Scotch-Irish in her features; the lines of her face were cut sure and clear, her eyes were dark and direct. She wore her hair pulled back into a thick braid that trailed down the back of her dress, almost to her waist. The red of her hair picked up the sunlight and glowed like fire.

Like Herbert Johnson, she was filthy. Her ankle-length dress, and the shortblouse she wore over it, were covered with dirt and stains. Her skirt had been snagged in so many places that she had given up mending it by the fire at night. She had an extra dress in her traveling sack, tied to the saddlehorn, but she wanted to save that for special.

It surely was hot, Maggie thought. And quiet. She was amazed at how deathly still the forest could be on afternoons like this. The only sound was the monotonous creaking of the leather packsaddles and the labored breathing of the horses as they plodded up the mountain trail.

Maggie thought she would give almost anything for a drink of water. Up ahead, through the shimmering heat, she could see Herbert Johnson riding along, hunched-over and hang-boned in the saddle, just as he had for the last fourteen days.

He didn't seem hot or tired or thirsty. He never did. He just rode. It didn't seem to occur to him that Maggie might be uncomfortable. By now, Maggie realized that Herbert Johnson wasn't particularly interested in her comfort. To the old mountain tinker, she knew she was just another piece of baggage to be carried up over the mountains for profit, no different from the iron pots or kegs of gunpowder carried on the backs of his pack-animals.

Thoughts passed like dark clouds through Maggie's mind. At times she wished she had never come to this wild, miserable place. For a while there she thought that if she could just lay down in the shade and drink a dipper of cool well water, if she could just be allowed to do that, she would give up this whole crazy scheme of hers and go back to Philadelphia. But there was no sense thinking that now. If she was thirsty, it was her own fault. She had forgotten to fill her water bottle at the spring that morning. She surely regretted that now.

Then Maggie heard something. It was the musical sound of running water. Up ahead she saw a stream, cascading down the mountainside and emptying into a shallow pool by the side of the trail. Mr. Johnson was already leading the horses over to drink. Maggie's animal followed right along.

Maggie slid down from her horse, gathered up her skirts and knelt at the edge of the pool, cupping big double handfuls of water up into her mouth. She dunked her entire head into the heavenly coolness of the water.

Once her thirst was satisfied, she filled her water bottle and corked it then lay back against a tree trunk, holding the cold bottle in her arms like a child might hold a precious doll. A breeze stirred, sending a wave of coolness through her wet hair. In that moment, she almost felt peaceful. She closed her eyes.

Then she heard the sound of Mr. Johnson's boots on the leaves as he walked near her. She opened her eyes. He was standing with his back to her, checking the cinch on the horse.

Maggie pulled herself up on one elbow.

"Is this where we camp for the night?" she asked.

Mr. Johnson still had his back to her. "No, Miz Callahan, gotta keep pushin'. We're nearly there now."

Maggie sat up straight. "Nearly there?"

Mr. Johnson turned to her and nodded. "Jest about. Once we top this mountain we'll go along the ridgeline for a ways then drop down through that mountain pass and I figure we'll ride into the Great Valley by nightfall."

Maggie couldn't believe her ears. Just when it seemed to her that the trails would go on forever, the old tinker was telling her that the journey was almost over. Suddenly the thirst and the dirt and the weariness didn't matter anymore. They were almost there.

They were bound for Penn's Valley which lay just north of the seven mountain ranges in the wild country of Central Pennsylvania. This was a valley so large and so impressive that on some of the old maps it was called simply "The Great Plains." The Great Plains. Ah, the many times Maggie had repeated that phrase to herself.

The Great Plains was where Maggie's new life lay. It was there that her Irish Aunt Franny and her Uncle Thomas had built themselves a homestead on forty acres of uncleared land. That would be Maggie's new home.

After the horses had drank their fill and rested, they mounted and began plodding up the trail again. Maggie's thoughts flew ahead of them. She would be sitting down to dinner with her Aunt Franny's laughter and secrets, just as they had in the good days in Philadelphia. After all Maggie had been through, it would be good to be safe and secure and cared-for for a while.

She had come nearly 200 miles in the last fourteen days and Maggie was ready to leave the life on the trail behind her. More than that, she was ready to leave her whole past behind. She wanted the dark memories of Philadelphia to stay back on the other side of the Susquehanna, where they belonged. For the first time in days, she was glad she had run away.

Just as the evening was coming on, Herbert Johnson reined his horse to a stop and swung around in the saddle. He shouted back along the packstring, loud enough for Maggie to hear.

"There she be, Miz Callahan: The Great Plains."

Maggie nudged her horse and rode up to where Mr. Johnson sat. Through the mountain pass before them,

Maggie saw a green and lovely valley, shadowed and peaceful in the evening light. This was the valley she had dreamt about for so long. It lay before them like a broad, flat map. Here and there she could see the curling plumes of chimney smoke, rising from the individual homesteads. Somewhere down in the valley, she heard a dog barking. Far in the distance, another range of mountains, purple in the evening light, stretched across the horizon.

Johnson clucked to his horse and they rode down into the valley, to a place where several trails came together. The tinker halted the packstring, swung down and walked back to Maggie.

"Come down off that horse now, Miz Callahan."

Puzzled, Maggie obeyed.

Mr. Johnson began to work at the strings that held her traveling sack to the horn of the saddle.

"This here's the forks of the trail," he was saying, "That trail to the west—just a footpath, really—that takes you up along the mountainside to where your Aunt Franny's cabin sets. This other trail—this one to the north—heads out along the valley to General Potter's place, that's where I'm headed. Now you take that trail up along the mountainside and you'll be at your Aunt Franny's door in less'n a mile."

"Now, wait a minute," Maggie said. "I thought you

were going to take me there."

"Never said that," Mr. Johnson replied, "said I'd bring you to the Great Valley. Here you be. Now I have business at Potter's tonight and you've slowed me down aplenty already."

He unlashed Maggie's traveling sack from the horn and let it drop on the ground. He tied the horse's reins to the animal before it. Then he walked to his own horse, mounted and rode away, as silent as can be, with nary a goodbye.

Maggie was thunderstruck. If she could have done anything to stop him, she would have. But she had already given him her mother's jeweled necklace in payment and there was certainly no point in chasing after him on foot. So she just stood, watching the packstring disappear down the horsetrail.

Maggie stood for some time, collecting her wits. She looked up the trail that hugged the mountainside. Then she looked at the sun, dipping low in the sky. It would be dark before long. A dark shadow of fear began to creep across her heart.

Then she brightened. After all, hadn't she come nearly 200 miles in the last two weeks? Hadn't she ridden the weary horsetrails and spent the night in mosquito-infested campsites along the way? She guessed, after all that, she could walk the last mile by herself. She swung her bag up on her hip and started up the trail.

The path took her up along the mountainside, through a thick hemlock woods. The trees rose like dark columns all around her. The heat of the day had lifted now, replaced by a cooling quietness.

Suddenly the silence was broken by the caw-ing of a pair of crows who flew over the treetops, warning the rest of the forest that she was coming. Maggie tilted her head back and smiled. It was then that she realized she had left her bonnet tied to the saddlehorn of the horse. But that didn't matter now, Franny would help her make a new one.

She walked for some time. Then, up ahead, through the trees, she saw a clearing of land on the shoulder of the mountain. In the center sat a modest log cabin. It was just as Franny had written about in her letters: walls of solid hewn logs, a hemlock bark roof and a real stone chimney. The front door was standing open, as if in welcome.

Maggie suddenly felt a terrible weight lifted from her. She was home now! She was really home! She dropped her bag and dashed out into the clearing, knowing that in a moment she would be swept up into the warm and welcoming arms of her Aunt Franny.

She burst inside the cabin—and stopped cold. What

she saw made her heart turn to ice.

The cabin was empty.

There were a few broken pieces of crockery laying around on the dirt floor. A torn piece of blanket hung from the rafters overhead. Branches and leaves had been blown in through the open door and were piled deep in the corners of the room. Maggie could tell that no one had lived there for a long time.

Maggie walked outside, unable to believe what she was seeing. There weren't more than a few armloads of firewood in the woodpile. Out back she could see where a space had been cleared for a garden. But nothing stood there now but a few of last year's dried cornstalks. They rustled in the wind and made a lonely sound.

Knowing it was a foolish thing to do, Maggie cupped her hands around her mouth and shouted off into the forest: "Franny? Franny? Uncle Thomas?" But her voice just died away in the stillness.

Maggie looked down. An old wooden bucket lay on it's side in the weeds. She turned it over and sat down on it. She put her chin in her palm.

Then a bright thought flashed into her mind. Maybe the neighbors would hear her cries and come up to fetch her. Maybe they would know where Franny was. Then she remembered from Franny's letters that the nearest neighbors were the family at the mill down along Sinking Creek and that was over a mile away.

Then a stiller, darker thought crept into her mind: Maybe her cries would attract other things: Mountain lions, black bear, maybe even a traveling hunting party of Iroquois Indians. For the first time since she had left Philadelphia, Maggie felt genuinely afraid.

It was then that she had the eerie feeling that she was being watched. She felt as though someone was behind her. She spun around and there, standing just a few paces away, was the wildest-looking man she had ever seen in her life.

He stood among the waving corn, stock still. At first she thought he was an Indian. Then she noticed that he had a long grey beard that trailed down the front of his hunting shirt. He was very old. He was dressed entirely in smoke-stained buckskins. A red-handled tomahawk and a sheath knife with a deer antler handle were thrust into the woven sash he wore at his waist. Hanging at his right side was his hunting pouch and powder horn. Clasped in his hands was a Pennsylvania longrifle, slanting up and away into the darkness. His hair was shoulder-length, grey and unruly. On his head was a cap made from black bear fur, with a single red-tailed hawk feather that tossed in the breeze as he stood watching her.

But it was his eyes that scared her the most. Peering out from under bushy eyebrows, they were sharp and angry. And cold as grey river ice.

Chapter Two

The old man stood there for a long time, staring at her. She was too frightened to move. When he finally spoke, his voice came out loud and gruff, like the growl of an old bear.

"Are you a crazygirl?" he asked.

Maggie would have spoke, but she couldn't get any voice up out of her throat so she just shook her head.

"Well, tell me this," he said, "if you're not a crazygirl, what're you doin' hollerin' off inta the woods like a crazy-girl for?"

Maggie managed to get some voice out of her throat this time, but it came out quavery and meek.

"Well," she started, "I was all by myself here and I was hoping someone would hear me if I shouted just as loud as

I could—"

"I heared you," the old man said, cutting her off, "and so did all the deer on the mountainside." He set the butt of his rifle down on the ground and pointed with his chin to the high ground.

"Jest covered with deertrails up there. Them deer come down through this clearing every evenin' at about this time. Come to drink at that spring over there. So, knowin' that, I been waitin' by that spring, waitin' for a good long time, bein' jest as quiet as I kin be, hopin' the forest would send me a deer tonight. Then some crazygirl comes along and starts shoutin' off inta the woods. Now don't that jest beat it with a stick?"

Maggie swallowed hard. "Well, I'm sorry. I didn't realize—"

"Where you from anyways, to be so uneducated?"

"From Philadelphia."

"Well, go back there. We don't need any crazygirls hollerin' off inta the woods around here."

Maggie took a deep breath. "But you don't understand. You see, my name is—"

"I don't care what your name is," the old man hissed, "you don't go shoutin' off inta the woods like that. Ruins the huntin'."

"I wish Franny were here," Maggie said to herself.

"What would you know about Franny Callahan?," the old man asked.

"That's what I've been trying to tell you. I'm Franny's niece, Maggie. I came here to live with her. Came all this way and now it looks like she's not here. Do you know where she is?"

The old man shook his head and chuckled. "Now don't that beat it with a stick. You're Maggie, eh? She spoke about you. Why didn't you say so in the first place?"

"Well, I tried to, but everytime I—"

The old man raised his hand. "Now, that's alright, you don't have ta explain, I sp'ose you're kinda turned inside out about all this. Well, I'll give it to you as di-rect as I ken. Your Aunt Franny and Uncle Thomas pulled up stakes and headed out to the Ohio Valley about four months ago, jest after the spring thaw."

Maggie drew a hand across her brow. "Oh, what a relief. Then you do know where they are. Just tell me where they went and I'll find my way out there and meet them."

The hunter shook his head. "Fergit that idee, girl. You could wander over that territory your whole life and never find 'em. When folks go west like that, they're gen'rally gone for good, never ta be seen again."

"Well what am I going to do?"

"Do? Well, girl, there's only one thing to do. We're jest gonna have ta set out tomorrow and I'm gonna have ta traipse you back downstream to the Susqueyhana, get you on a boat back to Philadelphy, where you belong. Thomas and Franny were like brother and sister to me, I'll do what I ken to see you back safely."

"But I can't go back," Maggie protested, "I haven't got anything to go back to."

"No fambly?"

Maggie shook her head. "Mama and Papa died of the fever three weeks ago. Had no brothers or sisters. Why, Franny's my only living relative."

"Well, only livin' relative or not, you got to go back. No place fer a civilized girl like you out here. So back you go, I don't want to hear any more about it." The old man scratched his chin-whiskers. "I jest got one question."

"What's that?"

"How in Lucifer's name did you get out here in the first place?"

Maggie sighed. "That's a long story."

The old man pushed his cap back on his head. "Well, I got all night. Nothin' to do now that the deer been run off."

The hunter slapped his leg. "But listen now, we can make jaw music about this later. You hungry?"

Maggie nodded. She was suddenly very hungry. Mr. Johnson's cooking hadn't been anything to rave about. The cornmeal mush he had made at dawn still lay like a dollop of lead in her stomach.

The hunter glanced around the clearing. "Well, we'll go inside and pull together a meal. You get that bucket yer settin' on and fetch us up some water from that spring over there. I'll go inside and strike us up a fire."

When Maggie returned to the cabin with the heavy bucket of water, she could see the old man knelt down by the hearth, laying out his fire-making gear: a chunk of flint, a bar of striking steel, a square of charred cotton cloth, and a handful of tinder made from the fluffed up inner bark of the willow tree. He had already built a small pyramid of hemlock twigs in the fireplace, ready to receive the fire when he had it going.

Maggie watched intently as he placed a thumb-nail sized square of charred cloth on the top of the flint, holding it down with the thumb of his left hand. He struck the edge of the rock a glancing blow with the steel bar. A shower of sparks flew up into the darkness. One landed on the char cloth and began to glow orange. The old man picked up the tinder bundle and carefully inserted the glowing cloth into its center. Then he held the tinder aloft and blew. Smoke began curling up and a moment later, the bundle burst into flames. He tucked the flaming bark in among the hemlock twigs. Instantly the fire crackled to life. He added larger twigs then branches. Then he turned to Maggie and said one word: "Wood."

She ducked outside and brought in all the wood she could scavenge from the woodpile. She went back out and fetched her traveling bag which lay at the edge of the clearing, where she dropped it. When she came back inside, she was glad for the firelight. The cabin seemed almost cheerful now.

In no time the old man had prepared a simple meal of hot sassafras tea and jerked deer meat. He found a wooden bowl on the floor, filled it with tea and passed it to Maggie. She took the bowl in both hands and drank. It tasted hot and strong. She sat back against the cabin wall and drank the rest of the tea, and chewed hard on a strip of jerky he handed her.

"A body travels these mountains by hisself for so long, he gets hungry for talk," the old man was saying. "You mind conversin' for a while?"

Maggie smiled. "No, I don't mind." She was a little hungry for talk herself. Herbert Johnson hadn't been much of a conversationalist.

"So tell me how you come to this valley." He asked.

"Came by horseback," Maggie said. "First across the

level road west from Philadelphia to Lancaster then on to Paxtang on the banks of the Susquehanna River. We crossed at Clark's Ferry then headed up the west bank to the mouth of the Juniata River. We ferried across and kept to the north bank of the Juniata right up into the mountains. We rode up over the mountain ridges, all seven of them and came down into the Great Valley just about sundown tonight."

"You keep sayin' 'we.' Who'd you come with?"

"A man by the name of Herbert Johnson, mountain tinker."

The old man nodded. "I've heared the name. But how'd you get hooked up with him? That is, if you don't mind me askin'."

"No. I don't mind," Maggie said in a weary voice, "I guess it can't do any harm to tell you.

"When Mama and Papa died, some folks from the church said they'd take me in as a hired girl and I could work for my keep. Do kitchen and garden work. Which would have been alright. And I was ready to go, too. But as I was packing up, I ran across Franny's letters she had sent since she moved out here.

"Franny and I were always real close. When Mama took sick years ago, Franny came to live with us in Philadelphia. Meanwhile Uncle Thomas came out here to

lay out a homestead. Few years later Franny came out to join him.

"That's when the letters started to come. Maybe two or three times a year, Franny would pay Herbert Johnson to carry me a letter when he came back to Philadelphia for re-supply.

"And, oh, I used to live for those letters. From the first time that I heard about this valley, I wanted to come out here and live with Franny.

"Anyway, I found these letters while I was packing up and I realized that I didn't want to move into some stranger's house and be a hired-out girl. I wanted to come out here and live with Franny. She was the one I felt closest to anyway. With mama so sick all the time and papa away so much, it was almost as if Franny was both mother and father to me.

"I remembered that one time Mr. Johnson told me that if I ever wanted to pay him to carry a letter back to Franny I could always leave word at the stable where he kept his horses. So I went down there and found him. Just by luck he was just about to leave on another trip west. So I talked him into bringing me out here. He said I'd have to pay him real well because of the added risk of transporting a run-away. So I did. I gave him my mother's wedding necklace — real jewels, you know. He said that would be alright. We loaded up and slipped out of town that night.

"So, you see, I really can't go back to Philadelphia. I guess they figure me like lost property. I think they'd whip me good if they could get me back now."

The old man warmed his moccasins by the fire.

"That was very brave, girl, takin' things inta yer own hands like that," he said, "but takin' a whippin' would be better'n starvin' or freezin' ta death up on this mountainside. So back you go, girl, and that's all there is to it."

Maggie decided to let the matter rest for now.

"I never even asked your name," she said.

"I'm just an old man," he said, "I don't need a name anymore. But those who talk to me call me by my given name."

"What's that?"

"Jake Logan. That's the name my mammy give me. But most folks around here don't care to talk to me anyway."

"Why's that?"

The old man laughed to himself. "You could say I'm a mite unpopular around here. The Scotch-Irish, they're settled folk. They don't take to wild men or wild critters, us that's been trampin' this valley long before they laid eyes on it. See, they plan to civilize this country and that kinda thinkin' doesn't leave much room for people like me.

"'Course your aunt and uncle were never that way. No, they were folks that knew how to live and let be. They were friends—I'd say the only friends I had in this valley." Jake settled back against the cabin wall. "Had many a fine meal inside these walls," he said. "Many a fine meal. Your aunt was a fine woman, you know. Likely, she still is. She sure had a way with people. Why, even the most cantankerous souls would warm up to her. That was partly 'cause of the way she was. And partly because of the bread a'course."

"What do you mean?"

"Well, Franny was known far and wide for that bread of hers. She would bake up that Callahan bread and people would just flock to it. Why, people'd move heaven and earth for that bread. Got to be so them loaves was good as money in these parts. Franny would bake 'em up and trade 'em for things she and Thomas needed. Many's the time I brought 'em squirrels and rabbits ta exchange fer that bread.

"No, we never had a bread like Franny's, not before or since. It rised up light and airy and thick-crusted at the same time. Made a man's mouth glad to chomp inta!"

The old man's lips began to work reminiscently.

"She was like a sister," the man said quietly, "the way she listened to folk's troubles and pains and baked the bread for 'em. Some people called her The Bread Sister, because that's just what she was. She was like a sister to everybody."

The old man had a far-away look in his eyes. Then he came out of it and turned his gaze to Maggie. She had been sitting wide-eyed, taking in every word.

Jake suddenly felt embarrassed, as though he had talked too long and too openly with this young girl. He suddenly slapped his buckskinned thigh and stood up.

"Well, now," he said, "We best get some sleep. We have to make tracks tomorrow. I'll set out first thing in the morning' and get us some meat for the trip—be back by noon at the latest. You stick close to the cabin 'til I get back. You can sleep in here by the fire, I'll bed down outside under the stars. That smoke will keep most of the bugs off you."

He gathered up his rifle and hunting pouch and stepped silently out into the darkness, leaving the door open behind him.

Maggie settled back against the cabin wall. It had been a long day and she was very tired. Through the open doorway, somewhere up along the mountainside, she heard the lonely call of a night bird, but she had no way of knowing what kind it was.

Chapter Three

Maggie lay back on the dirt floor by the hearthfire and fell asleep—fell into the deep sleep that weary people know—the sleep that gives way to dreams.

She dreamt that she was back in her parent's house in Philadelphia. Her father was away at sea, as he often was. Her mother, who was very ill, was asleep in her big bed upstairs.

Maggie was sitting before the hearthfire in the kitchen with her Aunt Franny. In the dream, Maggie could see her aunt sitting there—a tall, sturdy woman with a sure, strong way about her. Her red, red hair was twisted up into a bun she wore at the back of her head. The firelight flickered across her face, showing the lines that living had put there.

Maggie knew this dream. It was one she often had. It was the remembrance of something that had happened years before, something that had changed the girl's life forever.

Franny dried her hands off on her apron and took a deep breath before she spoke.

"Maggie," she said in her rough Irish brogue, "there's somethin' I've been meanin' to tell ye: I'm goin' away very soon...and I don't know that I'll ever be back."

Maggie smiled, as if she were hearing a joke. "What do you mean? You've always lived here. And you always will. You've lived here as long as I can remember."

"No, dear, it only seems that way. The time's really been very short. Now it's time for me to go."

Maggie began to realize that her aunt wasn't joking.

"Now you remember your Uncle Thomas," Franny went on, "You'll remember how he came over from Ireland on the boat with me and you'll remember that he went west two years ago to build a homestead on the frontier? You'll remember all that, won't you Maggie?"

The girl nodded slowly.

"Well, I got a letter from him this mornin' and he wants me to come over and join him when the spring thaw comes. He's got us a cabin on forty acres of land out there. And, Maggie, I have to go. 'Tis two year now since I saw my husband and I want a little farm of me own. I know that's hard for a little girl to understand. But maybe in time ye will. What's that look on your face now, dear?"

"I was just thinking," Maggie answered, "I was just thinking how different this house will be without you here. With papa gone so much and mama weaker than ever and just me here alone." Maggie began to cry. "I don't want to be here alone. Don't leave me, I want to go with you." She buried her head in the older woman's lap. Franny gently stroked the girl's hair.

"I know, dear, I know. If you were my own, I'd take ye with me in a minute. Don't think I haven't thought about it. But when I'm gone, your mother will need you more than ever. And, sure the frontier is no place for a young girl like yerself. Ye'll be wantin' to be near parties and dances before long now. There's none of that out there, just hard work Maggie. And, Good God, if somethin' ever happened to ye, yer mother would never forgive me."

"I don't care about all that," Maggie said, "I just want to go with you."

"Now, don't go on like that," Franny said. She took Maggie by the shoulders and held her firm, looking into her eyes.

"'Tis not the end for me and you, sure. I'll write every so often. And I want ye to know where ere ye go, I'll always be there in spirit. Won't ye remember that, Maggie?"

The girl nodded, tears rolling down her cheeks.

"Now," Franny said briskly, "I've got somethin' here for ye, sort of a goin' away present, from me to you."

Franny reached down into the bosom of her dress drew out an old leather pouch about the size of Maggie's fist, which hung around her neck by a leather thong. Franny held the pouch up in the firelight.

"Inside this pouch," Franny said, "is the most precious thing I can give ye. 'Tis somethin' that's been in the family many years. 'Tis the Great Callahan Spook Yeast."

Maggie wrinkled her brow. "I never heard of this before."

"Rightly so, dear. You never heard because 'tis our family secret."

"Spook Yeast," Maggie repeated the phrase, "Why's it called that?"

Franny laughed, "That's what me mother, God rest her, always used to call it. Because it's got a life of it's own, I suppose, like a spook."

"What's it good for?" the girl asked.

"Good for? To bake bread, o'course. I never showed ye this before but the spook yeast is the secret to bakin' the Callahan bread that you know so well. This bakin' secret has been passed down by the women in our family since

God knows when. And now 'tis time for you to learn, Maggie. Ye come by it honest, yer a Callahan yerself."

Maggie's eyes glowed with wonder.

"'Tis the yeasties inside this pouch that do the trick," Franny was saying. She dipped her fingers into the pouch and pinched off a roll of what looked like bread dough. She held it in her palm by the firelight.

"A loaf of bread without spook yeast is just as hard and flat as a brick. 'Tis a livin' thing, Maggie. If ye add a cup of this spook yeast to yer bread dough, the yeast creatures start workin' in the dough and the bread comes to life too."

"Smells sour." Maggie said.

"Aye, 'tis the smell of the yeasties workin'."

"What's it made from?" Maggie asked.

"The original Callahan Spook Yeast was nothin' but flour and water allowed to sour in the heat. That starts the yeasties to growin'. But this mixture has gained somethin' more by bein' passed down all those years. 'Tis the aging that's made the spook yeast what it 'tis. Some say ye can trace this yeast back for four generations in the Callahan family. And 'tis still goin', still alive."

"But why do you wear it around your neck like that?" Maggie asked.

"Because, dear, the yeasties are livin' things, ye got to

keep 'em warm. Too much heat kills them, too much cold puts them to sleep. The warmth of your body is just right. So I wear it around me neck, as all the Callahan women have, to keep it safe and warm as it should be.

"'Tis the closest thing the Callahans have to an inheritance, Maggie. And now 'tis time it came to you."

Franny reached into the pocket that hung at her apron and pulled out another leather pouch which looked like hers except that it was new.

As Maggie watched, Franny pinched out half of her own spook yeast and combined it with a cup of flour and water she had mixed and set by the fire. The tangy sour aroma of the spook yeast began to fill the kitchen. To Maggie it seemed as though she was watching magic at work.

Franny rolled the doughy mixture into a ball and placed it in Maggie's pouch then pulled the drawstring tight.

"Come sit by me here, Maggie," Franny said. The older woman held the pouch by the leather thong and settled it down over Maggie's head so the pouch lay like a necklace on the girl's chest. Maggie reached up and felt the pleasant roundness and fullness of the bag in her hand.

"It feels alive." she said.

"Aye," Franny nodded. 'Tis, dear, 'tis. Keep it safe

around yer neck and the life of the bread will never leave ye. I'll teach ye the bread bakin' secrets before I leave, dear. Take care of it and ye'll get many a loaf of bread out of that pouch. I have a feelin' that the bread bakin' will give ye a place in the world, Maggie. 'Tis somethin' of strength I can leave ye. So follow your nose, Maggie—"

"I know," the girl said, "I know what you always say: 'Follow your nose—and don't be afraid of nuthin'.'"

"Rightly so, Maggie," Franny said. Then she stopped for a moment and thought. "'Tis the rule I've lived by all me days. But that doesn't mean the same will work for you. 'Tis up to ye to make yer own rules, then stay to them. That's not always as easy as it sounds.

"You see, Maggie, you and I are different. The adventurous life is not for you. Yer a timid soul, Maggie, but ye got the strength of the Callahan's within ye.

"I've got the notion that someday ye'll be put to the test, like God tests us all. I think the most important thing for you to learn is not to *follow* your nose, as I have, but to look *past* your nose, to really *see* what yer lookin' at. Does that make any sense to ye?"

Maggie nodded.

"'Twill make more sense as time goes by," Franny said.

Then the dream faded away.

When Maggie next opened her eyes she found herself lying on the dirt floor in the cabin up on the mountainside.

In the eerie moments between sleeping and waking, Maggie wasn't sure whether she had just been with Franny or not. Then her head cleared and she realized that it had all been a dream and that Franny was out somewhere west, hundred of miles away.

Maggie looked outside. It was very dark. Dark as midnight. Seeking some light to comfort herself, the girl picked up a dead Hemlock branch, with the dried needles still clinging to it, and tossed it onto the glowing embers of the fire. The branch burst into fire. The flames leaped and danced on the cabin walls.

Maggie sat back against the wall and looked over the cabin. It was as though she were seeing it for the first time. Even in its run-down state, she could tell that Franny had once lived there. Franny's hand and eye for detail were everywhere.

The entire western wall was dominated by a huge stone fireplace Uncle Thomas must have built to Franny's careful specifications. The main chamber of the fireplace allowed plenty of room for hanging stewpots or setting up a roasting spit that could be used to turn and brown a duck over the coals.

Then Maggie spotted Franny's bake oven—a square chamber set into the rock wall. Maggie knew how carefully it had been constructed. It was similar to the one they'd used in Philadelphia. She knew the inside was bee-hive shaped and that the inner walls were plastered with clay, baked to rock hardness. She knew the bricks that formed the floor and walls of the oven were carefully made from pressed clay gathered from the creekbank. She knew all this without having to look inside.

Maggie rose and walked across the room, placing her

hand on the rough stone around the oven. Then she saw Franny's peel, standing propped-up in the shadowy corner, just as the older woman had left it. Her hand reached for it. It felt good and smooth to the touch. Uncle Thomas must have carved it from hard maple. Maggie knew that this long-handled, paddle-like tool was what Franny had used to lift her bread loaves in and out of the baking oven.

It was an eerie feeling holding Franny's peel like that. It was almost as though she felt the physical presence of her aunt nearby. Then the dream flashed into her mind. And she remembered Franny's words.

"Look past my nose," she said to herself, "now what's that supposed to mean?"

Her eyes fell on her traveling sack which lay against the cabin wall. She thought about how carefully she had packed it the night they had left Philadelphia. She had included things she thought she would need—an extra change of clothes and a few cooking provisions. But she had never gotten to use any of them. She sighed at the thought of carrying that heavy bag all the way back to Philadelphia with her.

She realized that the heaviest thing of all was the ten-pound bag of wheat flour she had brought, figuring to make bread on the trail. She thought about the other provisions that would go to waste—the bag of salt, the crock of honey. She thought about her bread knife, sharpened and stowed away in its canvas sheath—all things that wouldn't be used.

Suddenly Maggie really did see what she was looking at. She looked down at the peel in her hands, then back at the traveling bag.

"No," she thought to herself, "it won't go to waste. I've got everything here I need to bake bread. I'll carry that flour back as bread loaves."

From there on out, Maggie moved without really thinking. Her hands and mind did all the things that needed to be done, as though she were guided by some strong inner force.

She threw another branch on the fire and set to work. She knew that she must first mix her spook yeast starter. Maggie dipped into her pouch and pinched out a generous ball of spook yeast, added a few drops of honey and set it to ferment by the fire. She mixed her bread dough right in the flour bag by adding some water from the bucket and kneading it with her hands.

She took her clean apron out of the bag and spread it across an old wooden box. She dusted the surface of the apron with flour then rolled the huge ball of bread dough out onto it. The yeasty smells of the starter had begun to fill the cabin. Maggie thought of nothing but the bread. She added the spook yeast to the dough, knowing the life of the yeasties would now sink into the dough. She rolled it into a big ball, covered it with her apron, and set it near the hearth to rise.

Maggie suddenly felt tired. She lay down on the floor by the hearth and fell instantly asleep, knowing she would be rising early to stoke the baking fire.

At dawn Maggie began her baking fire by scraping a few glowing coals onto a piece of wood and carefully transferring the embers to the bake oven. She used all the wood laying around the cabin to build on that fire until it was a roaring blaze. When she went outside for more wood, she saw no sign of the old man. She knew he must have gone for hunting already.

When Maggie piled on the split hardwood, the flames shot up the flue with a roaring sound, like wind howling on a winter night. It was good, Maggie thought, she knew she needed to get the bricks inside the oven red-hot before the bread could be baked.

While the fire roared, Maggie checked her dough. It had risen overnight, as the spook yeast worked within it. She kneaded the bread down, using the familiar motions Franny had taught her so long ago. She felt the dough spring back under her hands, taking on a life of its own.

She felt Franny's spirit working with her on the dough. Then she remembered what her aunt had said: "I'll always be with ye in spirit, Maggie."

Maggie rolled the dough up into three perfectly round loaves then covered them and set them by the fire to rise a second time.

She was sweating freely now. The fire in the bake oven made the room quite hot, even though Maggie had the door propped open.

The fire was ready. Maggie used a branch to rake the burning wood from the oven and sweep it into the fireplace. The girl used a water-soaked rag wrapped around the end of a stick to swab the inside of the oven clean of dirt and ashes.

Maggie peered into the fierce heat of the oven. The bricks radiated an incredible amount of heat. The oven was ready. She used the last of the flour to dust the paddle of the peel and the floor of the oven so the dough wouldn't stick to those surfaces. The last thing she did before placing the loaves in the oven was to use her sharp knife to cut a cross into the top of each loaf. "To put the blessin' of God on the bread," as Franny would say.

She lifted the loaves onto the peel and, ever so gently, slid the loaves into the scorching heat of the oven. She lifted the wooden oven doorway from its place in the

corner and closed the oven up. She knew the loaves would bake quickly now, browning and doubling in size.

The girl wiped the sweat from her face with the corner of her apron. She walked out into the cool air. It was mid-morning by now and Maggie felt the sun coming up into the clearing, casting off the dark shadows made by the towering hemlocks. She sat on the doorstep to rest.

Then a thought floated into Maggie's mind. Franny had always told her that if something was troubling her and she couldn't find an answer on her own she should take her troubles to the bread. That was exactly what Maggie had done. She had taken her troubles to the bread. And in working the dough, an answer had come to her. It was so simple, she was surprised she hadn't thought of it before.

Chapter Four

Shortly before noon, Jake came back to the cabin with two squirrels and a string of fish slung over his back. As he was coming into the clearing, his nose began to twitch.

"That's the Callahan Bread," Jake said to himself. He quickened his pace. The old man came through the cabin door just in time to see Maggie pull the last of the rounded golden loaves from the bake oven. Jake's mouth dropped open.

"Girl," he said at last, "I didn't know you had the bread bakin' gift! Whyn't you tell me?"

"Well," Maggie said, "I didn't think it was important."

"Not important! Girl, nobody has had a decent taste of bread in this valley for months and you think it's not important!"

The old man knelt down and looked at the bread loaves like the old paintings show the wise men looking at the baby Jesus.

As Jake watched, Maggie sliced him a piece and handed it to him. He took the slice and held it under his nose with his eyes closed, bathing his weathered face in the fragrant smell. He took a bite, eyes closed, chewing like a man who had died and gone to heaven.

"It's the Callahan Bread," Jake said, "sure as any Franny ever baked."

Jake silently devoured slice after slice until he had eaten almost half a loaf.

"Don't eat so much," Maggie warned him, "hot bread's not so good for your stomach."

Jake patted his belly. "Right you are, girl, right you are. Jest tastes so good, a man fergits himself."

Maggie allowed herself a piece of bread. It did taste good hot, she had to admit.

"Jake," she said, "I've been thinking: What was it people used to call my aunt?"

The old man was brushing the crumbs off his beard.

"Oh, you mean 'The Bread Sister'."

"The Bread Sister." Maggie said the words to herself, to get the feel of them.

"And you said her bread was as good as money in this

valley, and that she would trade for things she needed?"

"That she would, girl. That she would. Like I said, people'd move heaven and earth for that bread."

"Well then, why don't I do that?"

The old man looked at her. "Do what?"

"What you said: Why don't I stay on here and bake the bread and trade for the things I need to live. I could take Franny's place as The Bread Sister."

"I was right," Jake said, "you are a crazygirl. Now, as much as I'd love ta have you here bakin' this bread regular, I still know in my bones that that would be a bad idee."

"But why?"

"Well, lotsa reasons," Jake said. "Oh, now your aunt could make it that way, it's true. But she had quite a few things in her favor, you know."

"Like what?"

"Well, first off, she didn't have to do it alone. She had a man, which you don't, and a good one at that.

"Second, Franny was a growed woman, which you ain't."

"I know about hard work," Maggie put in.

The old man shook his head, "Even allowin' that, yer still jest a girl and a lightweight at that. Franny knew how to do things you can't even imagine. She could skin a

squirrel, chop a load of firewood, even fire a flintlock if
need be. You know how to do all them things?"

Maggie shook her head.

"No, I didn't think so. And all that wouldn't be so bad,
girl. Except that you have no way of knowin' what it gets
like up in these mountains come winter. It ain't like settin'
up housekeepin' in Philadelphia. Why, I've lived in these
mountains for years now and I'm still thankful when
every spring rolls around and I'm here to see it.   "Now
you think you're gonna master all them skills I been
learnin' all my borned days? You think you're gonna learn
all that before the first snow flies?

"No, Maggie, it would be a cruelty to pretend you
could. Franny would skin me alive if she ever found out I
let you freeze er starve ta death up on this mountainside.
So back you go, bread bakin' er not!"

Just then a shadow fell across the doorway, blocking
out the morning light. The old man and the girl turned
and saw someone standing in the doorway.

He was huge. Not just tall, but broad and solid like an
oak barrel. Even though he was dressed simply in a
farmer's shirt, vest and knee breeches, Maggie noticed
that he had his hair carefully arranged into a fashionable
queue plaited down the back of his neck. His face was
flushed red and his eyes, peering through spectacles

perched on his nose, were wide and angry.

In his hand was a flintlock dueling pistol, pointed directly at Jake's chest.

"Don't move, Mr. Logan." His voice sounded overly loud and theatrical in the tiny cabin. He stepped over the doorsill and into the room. As he did, his spectacles slid down his nose and he had to poke them back up again. The big man shifted his eyes to Maggie. He motioned to her with his free hand.

"Well, child, don't just stand there like a duck in a thunderstorm, move over here by me, I'll protect you."

Maggie felt unable to move.

"Has he harmed you?" the man asked.

Maggie shook her head.

"Well, it's fortunate for you that I happened by. This man could have done you great harm. He is the only criminal who inhabits this valley and the only human danger we face. Except, of course, for the red savages."

It was then that the big man caught sight of the string of fish and squirrels hanging from the rafters, where Jake had left them.

"Ah," he said, "poaching again?" He gave a high, hysterical laugh that filled the cabin. "I've caught you red-handed, you rapscallion, and now you will receive the punishment you so richly deserve.

"I have among my papers at the house a formal complaint drawn up by the leading citizens of this valley. You seem to have a poor understanding of property rights. We are landholders in this valley now. That means that we own not just the land but everything upon it—the plants, the animals, the mineral resources.

"The days are over, Mr. Logan, when you can wander the valley at will, shooting animals and picking apples and frightening people with your rude and uncivilized ways.

"So, by the power vested in me as deputy constable, I will now escort you to General Potter's house where you will receive thirty lashes at the public whipping post."

Maggie cut her eyes back to see how Jake was taking all this.

"Better watch that pistol," Jake said evenly, "it could go off and hurt someone."

The big man glanced down at the pistol, then quickly back at Jake. It was then that his nostrils caught the scent of the bread.

"I must say, is that bread I smell?" he asked.

"Yes it is, Maggie spoke up. "I baked it. You see, my name is—"

"I don't care what your name is, young lady, you are safe with me. I can't help but wonder about the bread." His eyes fell on the loaves.

"These rounded, golden loaves, they remind me of Franny's bread." His eyes glazed over. He seemed to have forgotten the pistol in his hand. "Haven't had any bread here for—how long is it, now?"

Maggie stooped and sliced him a steaming chunk and carried it to him. The man popped it into his cavernous mouth and began chewing with his eyes closed.

It was at that moment that Jake made his move. He silently slid across the room, just two steps to the door, snatched up his rifle leaning against the wall, and was gone.

Maggie saw it all.

"Ah, yes," the man was saying, "food of the gods. I have always said to my good wife Maura, there is nothing like fresh-baked bread to make a house a ho--." He glanced around. "Now where is that rapscallion?"

He grew very red in the face and turned and dashed out the doorway. He glanced around the borders of the clearing.

"Logan!" he bellowed. "I know you're out there. I know you can hear me." He shook his fist at the treeline. "I swear to you that this is not the end. I swear, by the trust the citizens of this community have placed in me, I will bring you to the whipping post. There is justice in this valley!"

His oration finished, the man heaved a great sigh and stepped back into the cabin. He sat down on the doorstep and began wiping his forehead with an enormous handkerchief.

"He's eluded me again." the man said. Then he glanced up at Maggie and stood up rather formally.

"I know this all must be quite confusing to you," he said. "Allow me to introduce myself. I am Joseph McGrew. I own the mill down on Sinking Creek. I was Franny's nearest neighbor.

"When I saw the chimney smoke this morning, I thought Franny might be back. So I came up here to investigate. A deputy constable must pay attention to these things, you know. Public service, public service. You aren't hurt in any way then?"

Maggie shook her head.

"Good. Now perhaps you will answer some questions for me. Who are you and what brings you to this green and verdant valley?"

Maggie took a deep breath. "My name is Maggie Callahan and I came here from Philadelphia to live with my Aunt Franny—"

"Ah, yes, Philadelphia. I remember it well. My wife and I used to be on the great stage in Philadelphia." He sang a snatch of an aria, very loud and very terribly. "Unfortunately, we encountered a few hostile audiences. Maura and I were obliged to leave town on short notice."

He swept his arms in an impressive gesture.

"Then we turned our faces to the challenge of the frontier. We've built a home here in the savage wilderness. And this will be a great community someday. With banks and churches and schools. And places of culture, too. Where I can personally perform the works of the great

playwrights for the delighted audiences of the future. Now, of course, I'm heavily involved in the mill business—but that's only a phase in the great master plan. After all, don't you think there's as much good to be done in business and politics as in the arts?"

Maggie nodded.

Then McGrew clapped a hand to his forehead.

"But what am I thinking of? Here I am, rambling on, while you have needs that must be attended to. Come down to the house with me now. Any visitor is a treat to us. Especially a Callahan who brings such delicious breadstuffs to our table." McGrew suddenly stopped himself. "Forgive me. You don't mind bringing these to our table do you?"

Maggie shook her head. She was very confused by all of this. She remembered Franny had mentioned McGrew in her letters and said that he was a good man. So she gathered up the extra loaves in her apron and picked up her nearly-empty traveling bag. McGrew picked up the string of game.

"By the way," McGrew said, "You do know about your aunt and uncle moving on, don't you?"

Maggie nodded. "Jake Logan told me."

"Just as well," McGrew said, "I hate breaking bad news."

They walked down the path toward Sinking Creek. On the way, McGrew asked about Maggie's circumstances in coming to the valley. He talked about his theatre career. As they strolled along, he sang in a loud voice. Birds and squirrels scattered before him as he walked. Maggie wondered what Jake would say about McGrew's way of traveling in the woods. But then, she thought to herself, there were probably a lot of things the two men disagreed about.

Chapter Five

When Maggie first saw Sinking Creek, she was surprised at how small it was. In some places it was so narrow that a nimble person could easily leap across. But it was clear and ran with a musical tone.

They came into a clearing and she could see that the stream had been dammed into a pond. She could see the mill reflected in the still water of the pond. It was a huge impressive structure with an enormous wooden waterwheel.

As they walked, McGrew explained that the runoff from the pond was channeled down a long wooden chute where a steady stream of water fell onto the paddlewheel, turning it smoothly. The motion of the wheel turned the grindstones inside which ground rye and corn into flour and cornmeal. McGrew said in the winter the same power was used to run the up-and-down motion of a saw-toothed blade in the sawmill out back.

As they drew closer, Maggie could see the main house, set up away from the pond a bit. It was a tranquil scene.

"Let me show you my pride and joy," McGrew said hospitably. He took Maggie into the mill and she marveled at the maze of wooden cogwheels that turned the heavy grindstones. The mill was not operating at the moment. McGrew excused himself to climb up and check the works.

Maggie was so impressed by the massive wooden machinery that she didn't notice the little girl who had walked up beside her. Maggie turned and, suddenly, there she was, seemingly out of nowhere. She looked to be about eight years old. She was barefoot and wore a simple cloth dress. She had jet-black hair and very delicate hands and feet.

"Hello," Maggie said, "What's your name?"

The girl smiled. With great care, she slowly drew the letter "A" in the air with her finger. Then she drew another letter. An "N". Another "N". An "I". And an "E."

"Annie," Maggie said, "Your name is Annie."

Annie gave her a dazzling smile then reached out and firmly shook her hand.

Just then McGrew climbed down from the loft.

"Ah," he said, "I see you've met my daughter."

"She's very clever with her hands." Maggie said. "She spelt her name out in the air for me. But she must be very shy. I'd like to hear her voice."

"So would we," McGrew said sadly.

"What do you mean?"

"Our girl Annie can't speak or hear. Several years ago, she was involved in a terrible accident. Miraculously, the Lord spared her life. But, in his wisdom, he took from her the powers of speech and hearing.

"However, she is a bright girl. And she has devised her own ways of communicating. If you speak slowly, she can read your lips. And she has invented a sort of language of her own, with gestures and handsigns. I dare say, once you get on to her way of signing, you can speak with her about most anything."

Annie touched McGrew on the arm to get his attention. She made a series of graceful motions with her hands and pointed to Maggie.

"She wants to know where you're from and what you're doing here," he explained.

The big man slowly recounted Maggie's story. Annie watched, her eyes riveted to her father's lips. Maggie saw the waves of sadness begin to break across the little girl's face as she came to understand Maggie's predicament.

Annie touched her palm to her heart and shook her head.

"She says she feels sad for you." McGrew said. "But listen, no point in dwelling on all this now. What's done is done. You must agree to be our house guest for the night."

McGrew turned to Annie. "Take Maggie to the house, introduce her to your mother and ask her that we might have Maggie as our house guest tonight."

Annie nodded and took Maggie's hand in hers.

As they approached the house, Maggie could see that the McGrew's house was built on a much grander scale than Franny's cabin. The log walls were hewn flat and neatly fitted at the corners. There were two chimneys, one at each end and a real shingle roof.

As they came closer, a tall woman, dressed entirely in black, wearing a black bonnet that covered most of her face, stepped from the doorway and threw a kettle of filthy water into the weeds.

She heard them approaching and looked up. Her face was in shadow but beneath the ruffle of the bonnet, Maggie could see two dark, sharp eyes peering out at her. The woman simply stood with the kettle in her hands, staring at Maggie as though she had seen a ghost.

"This is Maggie..." Annie signed, "She came here from

Philadelphia and Papa says to ask can she stay here with us tonight."

Maggie shifted under the woman's gaze.

"Where's your bonnet?" the woman said at last. She spoke to Maggie in a voice that sounded like a whiplash.

"I lost it," Maggie admitted.

"Sensible girl wouldn't be out in the sun without a bonnet," Mrs. McGrew declared.

"Well," Maggie began, trying to sound friendly, "I know that. But, you see, my name is—"

"I already know your name," the woman snapped. She pointed to Maggie's clothes.

"Look at your dress. You look like you've been rolling in the dirt. I don't know why my husband insists on taking in every stray traveler in the valley. Well, you won't come in my house that way."

She turned to Annie and made hand motions for washing. Then, for Maggie's benefit, she said, "Take her to the pond. And scrub her good."

Mrs. McGrew turned her gaze back to Maggie. "I don't allow slovenliness in my house." Then she turned and was gone. Her words hung like icicles in the air.

Maggie went to the pond and washed herself with the harsh lye soap Annie brought. Then the younger girl poured a bucket of water over her head and she washed the traildust out of her hair. Annie had also brought her a simple sack dress. Maggie hadn't felt so clean in weeks. It felt good to sit by the pond with her eyes closed, letting the sun dry her as Annie's nimble fingers brushed out her hair and plaited it into two long braids that trailed down her back.

When they returned to the house, the family was prepared to sit down to supper. It was a simple meal, cold fish and corn, left-over from the bigger meal the family customarily ate at noon. But the meal was made grand by the addition of Maggie's bread.

McGrew took his place at the head of the table. Mrs. McGrew had taken off her bonnet now and Maggie could see from Mrs. McGrew's high cheekbones and graceful aquiline nose that she had once been a beautiful woman. But now, Maggie thought, her face looked pale and tired and very sad.

She glanced around the room and saw that Mrs. McGrew did keep a very clean house. The fireplaces at each end of the house were well-stocked with split firewood for cooking, the stone hearths were swept clean. Mr. and Mrs. McGrew's bed, which sat in one corner was neatly made with a comfortable quilt. Maggie saw the ladder going up to the loft overhead where she figured Annie slept.

Then Maggie saw something else. Sitting in the corner by the large bed was a hand-made cradle. In the cradle was a sleeping baby.

"Let us bow our heads," McGrew said and began to say grace over the meal. He had no sooner thanked the Lord for two or three things than the baby started awake and began screaming. Mrs. McGrew wearily left her place at the table and lifted the baby from its cradle. Maggie saw Mrs. McGrew open the front of her blouse and nurse the infant. As soon as the child began suckling, its cries quieted.

"Our little boy Lyons is quite ill," McGrew said, "he was a sickly child from the start and since then it's been just one illness after another. We've come very close to losing him."

McGrew bowed his head and finished his prayer.

"Now," McGrew said with an expansive smile, "let's share in the bounteous wonder of this bread."

Maggie carefully selected a fresh loaf and cut a large slice for each person. Mrs. McGrew put the sleeping baby back in the cradle and came to the table. Maggie watched as the three McGrews sat silently and ate the bread, eating quietly, as though making a sound would somehow interfere with the taste.

McGrew washed the last of his slice down with a mug

of cider.

"Well, Maura," he said. "It's the Callahan Bread now isn't it? Fine a loaf as ever Franny baked."

Mrs. McGrew nodded silently.

After the meal was over, Mrs. McGrew had Maggie do the washing up. While she worked, Maggie was conscious that the older woman was watching her every move.

That evening Maggie and Annie began to climb the ladder to the sleeping loft.

Then Maggie heard Mrs. McGrew's voice saying, "Maggie, come here."

Mrs. McGrew was sitting in her rocking chair by the hearth. She wore a light shawl over her shoulders against the cool of the evening. Her face looked tired and drawn.

"Joseph and I have talked over your situation," Mrs. McGrew began, "We are prepared to offer you a proposal which may be the solution to your problem, at least temporarily.

"I will begin by saying that I believe the wisest thing would be for you to return to Philadelphia immediately. You have no way of knowing the hardships life in these mountains can bring on. Unfortunately, you cannot make the trip alone and there is no one here who can spare the time to take you. So. Let me ask you: How do you plan to survive here?"

Maggie looked down at her feet. "I don't know, m'am."

The older woman took a deep breath. "I see. Well, harvest time will be on us soon and we can use an extra pair of hands around here. We are prepared to offer you room and board in exchange for your labor in this household until such time as you can return to Philadelphia, which will most probably be in the spring. Is that agreeable to you?"

Maggie nodded.

"Just as well," Mrs. McGrew said, "seeing as how you don't have much choice anyway. I want to make it clear at the outset that you are neither a guest or a boarder in this house. Your position will be the same as a bound-out girl's would be. You may consider yourself a servant, to put it in plain terms.

"Your duties will be to help me in the house and garden in whatever way I deem necessary. You will answer directly to me. There is to be no complaining to my husband. He has no authority in this household. Is that clear?"

Maggie nodded.

"Then let me ask you one more question: Are you the tearful type?"

Maggie shook her head. "Not really."

"Well, if you are, we'll find out soon enough. I must also

say that although Franny and I didn't always see eye-to-eye, she kept a clean house and minded her own business. You do the same and you'll not fare badly here. Any questions?"

Maggie shook her head.

"Very well. Go up and get a good night's rest. We begin boiling clothes right after breakfast."

"Thank you, Mrs. McGrew," Maggie said.

Maggie turned and climbed the ladder to the loft. Annie was sleeping peacefully on her straw mattress. Maggie found a blanket to roll up in. She lay there, staring at the rough boards overhead. Downstairs, she heard little Lyons cry.

She rolled over and peeked down through the slits in the board floor. Mrs. McGrew sat holding her child by the hearthfire, rocking. Maggie wondered what kind of strange, bitter woman she had bound herself out to. As Maggie peered down at Mrs. McGrew's face it occurred to her that, even suckling her tiny son, there was no tenderness in this woman's face, only a fierce and enduring sadness.

Chapter Six

Maggie thought she knew all about hard work. But whatever she had done in her life was nothing compared to what Mrs. McGrew expected of her. Maggie soon learned that a woman's life on the frontier wasn't anything to be envied.

All she saw was a continual stream of drudgery: washing, cooking, mending, hauling and chopping. All of it dirty and hard and exhausting. It was a lot to expect from a young girl. But Maggie noticed that Mrs. McGrew expected no less from herself. Mrs. McGrew went about the dreary tasks slowly, methodically, without a cheerful word or a smile, as though she was carrying some great burden.

But Annie was there to brighten the dark sadness that

Mrs. McGrew cast across their lives. Maggie and the little girl grew to be like sisters. Once a week Mrs. McGrew allowed Maggie to go up to Franny's cabin to bake up bread for the week. It was on those days that the girls felt free as birds and light as air. Sometimes, when Mrs. McGrew couldn't spare Annie, Maggie went to the cabin alone. It was at these times that Maggie felt Franny's presence strongly in the cabin. The solitude gave her the strength to go on.

Jake stopped by the cabin one day while Maggie was baking.

"Found yerself a home, have you girl?" he asked.

Maggie nodded. "I'll be staying around until the spring anyway, bound-out to the McGrew's."

"I figgered as much," Jake said. "And suits me fine so long's I kin get a taste of bread every now and again."

Maggie was glad to give him a loaf to carry away in his shoulderbag. Mrs. McGrew would never know and Maggie enjoyed seeing the old man, even if he was supposed to be dangerous.

The mill was especially busy that fall. Farmers in the valley grew corn and rye and brought their crops to the mill to be ground into cornmeal and flour. Since there was no coin money to be had, McGrew simply kept a portion of the grain in payment. He even set up a credit system which allowed him to be both businessman and politician, something he greatly valued. McGrew sought everyone's friendship. In most cases, he got what he wanted. He was an irrepressible, irresistible character who was as gay and full of jokes as his wife was somber.

One day the McWilliams family from downstream came by to unload a wagonful of corn. They had the noon meal together while they were waiting for the corn to be ground. Maggie served her bread.

Mrs. McWilliams and Maggie were helping Mrs. McGrew do the washing up when the neighbor woman complimented Maggie on her bread.

"You Callahan women certainly can bake," she was saying, "I wish I could do the same. But I just don't have the time. A bread like that would surely brighten up our meals."

"Well," Maggie offered, "If you like, I could bake up a few extra loaves for you. I go up to Franny's to bake every Saturday and it would be no extra trouble to do a few extra loaves this week. You could come by the mill and pick them up Sunday."

Mrs. McGrew, working nearby, stiffened.

Mrs. McWilliams beamed. "That would be wonderful, Maggie. Of course, I'd want to give you something for your trouble."

Maggie thought for a moment. "Well, you were saying that you dipped tallow candles last week, we could surely use some of those."

"Hold it," Mrs. McGrew said. "Don't be so free with that bread, Maggie. Remember that you are in my employ and that the fruits of your labor belong to me."

Maggie nodded. "I know that, Mrs. McGrew. But, like I said, it's no extra trouble for me and we do need the candles. Think of the work it would save us."

Mrs. McGrew nodded. "I'm not contesting that, Maggie. But this should be my decision, not yours. I have no objection to this bread trading so long as it doesn't interfere with your other duties and so long as you trade for things we really need, no foolishness."

"Of course," Maggie said.

Mrs. McGrew cast a frozen glance at Mrs. McWilliams then picked up a bucket and went out the door toward the pond.

"I can't understand why she's so rude," Mrs. McWilliams said after the other woman had gone. "If you were in my household, I'd treat you different, sure. I declare, Maura McGrew is the sourest woman I know."

Maggie nodded. "I just keep remembering something Mr. McGrew told me one time. He told me that sometimes you have to look really hard to see that she is being just as friendly and cheerful as she knows how."

Mrs. McWilliams laughed. "I suppose. But, you know, she wasn't always that way. When Maura and Joseph first came to this valley, they were the gayest couple you could ever wish to meet. But it's five years now that Sarah's in the grave and Maura still walks around like a woman in mourning."

Maggie asked: "Who was Sarah?"

There was a moment of uncomfortable silence. Then Mrs. McWilliams brushed it aside.

"Don't mind me, Maggie. Just foolish woman's talk is all. I've said too much already." Then she changed the subject.

Although she never asked anyone else about it, scarcely a day passed when she didn't wonder about Sarah. She noticed the McGrew's rarely talked about their early days in the valley and Maggie came to sense that there was some dark secret hidden there.

When the news of Mrs. McWilliams' deal with Maggie spread, other women followed suit and soon Maggie was baking twenty loaves a week for the neighboring families. The things the family got through trade—fresh meat, soap, cloth and tools—made their lives easier and so long as Maggie could do her bread baking in one day, Mrs. McGrew didn't object.

The summer ended. September came on. Joseph McGrew got a letter that fall from his sister Catherine in Lancaster. She proposed that she send her 19-year old son, John, out to apprentice to McGrew at the mill. Always eager for an extra hand, McGrew agreed.

It was on an overcast afternoon in early September that the packtrain carrying McGrew's nephew arrived in the valley. McGrew packed up the whole family in the wagon and went down to the forks of the trail at General Potter's house to meet him.

McGrew's mill and Potter's house were the two most important spots in that end of the valley. The mill was the center for business and Potter's house served as a combination fort and meeting place. In case of Indian trouble, the settlers had agreed to make a stand at Potter's fortified house. But Indians had made no trouble in years. For the most part, people were drawn to Potter's because it was located on a main trail and because Potter was an influential, energetic man who knew how to get things done.

When McGrew pulled the wagon up before the house, they could see two freshly-killed deer hanging from their hind legs on a tripod before the house.

"Looks like Potter's rifle has been true again," he said. "Maura, a taste of venison would be good this time of year. I believe I'll arrange a trade."

"Very well," Mrs. McGrew said, "But don't barter our lives away for it."

Just then John came striding out through the front door. McGrew got down from the wagon and went over to shake his hand.

"Good to see you, my boy, you've grown tall since I've seen you last, eh? Come and say hello to the family."

They walked toward the wagon.

"I believe you know everyone here except for our hired girl, Maggie Callahan."

John reached up to where Maggie sat in the back of the wagon and took her hand.

"Just as pretty as Uncle Joseph told me you'd be," he said, "I'm sure we'll be seeing a lot of each other." Then he winked.

Maggie drew her hand back. She took an instant dislike to this brash stranger.

Potter, a short powerful man, came through the doorway and motioned the men inside. "Have a drink before you leave gentlemen?"

McGrew smiled. "Come along my boy, you're about to get your first lesson in commerce on the frontier."

The men disappeared inside. Twenty minutes passed.

"Never did see them do any business without a jug of whiskey to wash the deal down," Mrs. McGrew said testily.

At that moment McGrew came through the open doorway, tripped over the doorsill and fell flat on his face. John stumbled out after him. He bent over the older man.

"Uncle Joseph, are you alright?" he asked.

McGrew scrambled to his feet.

"Of course, John. Must be those benches we were sitting on. Cuts off the blood flow to the legs, makes a man's knees go wobbly."

Potter had taken off his coat and rolled up his sleeves. "Let's get that deer loaded up," he said, "storm's on the way, I can feel it in my bones."

With some grunting and cursing, the men managed to load the deer up into the wagon. John climbed up into the wagon bed, pulled an old blanket over his head and was instantly snoring loudly. McGrew walked around and, after several tries, managed to vault himself up into the seat.

"Joseph McGrew," Mrs. McGrew said sternly, "you're drunk as a skunk."

McGrew drew himself up into the picture of mock dignity. "Maura," he said, "you cut me to the quick. I was merely—"

"I know exactly what you were doing." She glanced overhead, "If we hurry we'll make it home before the rain hits. Are you able to drive?"

"Of course, my dear." McGrew snapped the reins and they were off, headed down the rutted wagonroad toward Sinking Creek.

They had been traveling for less than ten minutes when McGrew fell asleep with the reins in his hands. He toppled backwards into the wagon bed and landed beside John and the body of the doe.

Mrs. McGrew made a desperate grab for the reins and managed to snatch them up before they fell under the wagon. She held little Lyons in the crook of her arm as she turned around in the wagon seat.

"Maggie," she said sharply, "come up here and hold Lyons."

Maggie crawled up into the seat and took the baby in her arms. A light, freezing rain began to fall. Maggie covered the baby's face with a blanket. She looked back over her shoulder and saw Annie moving around in the back of the wagon, unfolding an old blanket and using it to cover her father and her cousin against the rain.

Mrs. McGrew snapped the reins and they were moving again. The rain began to fall harder now, pelting them with stinging, cold drops. Maggie glanced up at the sky, water streaming down her face. The clouds looked grey and foreboding. Suddenly, a bolt of lightning cracked overhead. Thunder rolled like drums.

Maggie noticed that Annie had crawled forward in the wagon, coming up behind Mrs. McGrew. Annie started tugging on her mother's rain cloak. Annie's eyes were wide with terror. The little girl began sobbing hysterically. Her mouth moved, but no sound came out.

Then Maggie glanced over at Mrs. McGrew and she saw something she would never forget. Etched in the older woman's face were the same lines of fear. Any display of emotion would have been unusual for Mrs. McGrew, but Maggie wasn't prepared to see this hardened woman trembling in terror. She knew something must be deeply wrong, something she couldn't understand. Surely there was more to this than a simple lightning storm.

Annie grew so insistent in her pleading that Mrs. McGrew had to pull the wagon to a stop. She swung around, grabbed Annie by the shoulders and shook her violently.

"Stop that crying!" Mrs. McGrew shouted against the rain. Her voice was high and hysterical. "Don't you see? You're only making it worse. It won't be like last time! Annie?" she shouted, "Do you hear me?" Then the older woman caught herself, "No," she wailed bitterly, "of course you don't." Then she flung the girl back into the bed of the wagon where she fell sobbing beside her father.

Maggie turned to say something to Mrs. McGrew, to calm her down, but it was too late. The older woman had snapped the reins and started the horses down the muddy road at a brisk trot. The road was full of ruts and gully-washes and the wagon bounced so hard that Maggie had to brace her feet and hold onto the seat with one hand to keep from being tossed out.

Maggie couldn't understand why she was driving so fast. What was her hurry? A horse could slip and break a leg on a wet road like this.

Up ahead Maggie could see the place where the road forded Sinking Creek. This was normally an easy crossing through shallow water. But the pelting rain had swelled the creek into a muddy, raging torrent, near as deep as the wagon bed.

Mrs. McGrew saw the water too. She braced her feet and pulled back on the reins, bringing the speeding horses to a stop. Maggie thought that Mrs. McGrew would back the team up and turn around and head back to Potter's now. But she didn't do that. She just sat with the reins in her hands, her eyes fixed on the swirling waters like a woman in a trance. The roar of the water filled their ears.

A bolt of lightning fractured the sky overhead and jolted Mrs. McGrew into action. She lashed the reins and the horses sprang forward, dashing toward the creekbed.

"No," Maggie thought, "she's not going to try to run the stream!" But it was too late. The horses had already plunged into the stream, sunk in up to their withers. The rapids welled up around the wagon bed.

The left front wheel struck a rock, tipping the wagon to the right and for a moment they almost upset in the current. Maggie leaned back in the seat to keep from falling out and, as she did, little Lyons tumbled out of her

arms and disappeared into the water.

For a moment she was too stunned to move. Then something inside of her took over. She jumped over the side of the speeding wagon and disappeared into the rapids. Even though the water was only waist deep, she sunk in over her head and was swept a dozen yards downstream before she could find her feet and stand up. The cold of the water took her breath away and for a moment it seemed that she might drown herself. But she caught her breath and began thrashing around in the water looking for the baby. It seemed hopeless.

Then she saw him, about twenty yards downstream. A dead tree had fallen into the water and Lyon's clothing had snagged on one of the branches. The baby hung, just under the surface of the water, limp as a rag doll.

Maggie let the current take her over that way. With her hands, she managed to snap off the branch that held the baby.

Holding Lyons to her chest, she fought her way up through the shallows and onto the muddy bank. She lay him on his back in the mud and tore open his shirt, placing her ear to his bare chest. Nothing. No movement. No sound. Was he dead?

Then Maggie remembered something she had seen Franny do with a small baby years ago. She turned Lyons over with his head pointed down and gave him a sharp whack between the shoulder blades with the palm of her hand. The baby choked and vomited up a gaggle of water.

"That's it, Lyons," she said encouragingly, "come on, baby, breathe!"

She continued clapping the baby's back with her hand. More water came up. Then Lyons let out a piercing wail and began to cry. Maggie was never so glad to hear a baby scream. She turned him over and looked him in the face. His eyes were squeezed shut and his mouth was wide open, screaming for all he was worth.

"You did it, Lyons! You came back to us! You're alive!" she shouted.

Maggie glanced up the road and saw that Mrs. McGrew had pulled the wagon to a stop and was running down the road toward them.

Mrs. McGrew took the baby and held it tight and rocked it in the rain, wailing and sobbing. Maggie led her back to the wagon and drove the team the rest of the way home.

The men woke up just as they pulled up to the front door. While Maggie put the horses in the shed, the McGrew's stumbled inside and got a fire going. By the time Maggie trooped in, they were all wrapped in warm blankets, shivering by the fire.

She stripped off her wet cold clothing and wrapped herself up by the fire. No one spoke. They just stared at the fire with their teeth chattering, as though the very sight of the flames could bring the warmth back into their bodies.

Maggie felt a hand on her shoulder. It was Mrs. McGrew's.

"Death passed close by here today," the older woman said in a trembling voice, "you drove it away, Maggie. I won't forget that."

"It was nothing special," Maggie said, shivering, "I mean, anybody would have done the same for a baby."

Mrs. McGrew didn't say anything more. She just stared into the flames.

Maggie felt a death-shiver go through her body. Death had passed awfully close by that day.

Chapter Seven

The McGrew's never mentioned anything about the night of the lightning storm again. But it was apparent that something very elemental and very terrifying had happened there that night, something that Maggie only dimly understood.

Then, one day, quite accidentally, she stumbled across the secret.

John had loaded up a mule with two barrels of flour, coaxed the animal up the mountain trail to Franny's cabin. Maggie had gone along to see the cargo safely there.

"All this work I'm doing for you," John joked, "you ought to give me a cut of your bread-baking profits."

Maggie snorted. "Not much profit to speak of, John."

They were coming into the clearing now, bringing the mule around to the front door.

"How much you charge for that bread anyway?" he asked.

"I don't charge any set amount," Maggie explained, "I just trade for what I need."

John laughed. "That's no way to run a business."

"Just as well," Maggie returned, "I'm not running a business, I'm just living."

"That's a woman's talk for you now," John said, "haven't you got a headful of strange notions about the way the world works? Talk like that: reminds me of my cousin Sarah."

Maggie's ears pricked up. She tried to make her voice sound casual. "Sarah? Who's that?"

John was unlashing the barrels from the packsaddle.

"Oh she's long gone now. Been dead for years. But she was a spunky girl, I'll say that. She was Uncle Joseph and Aunt Maura's oldest daughter. And the apple of their eye, I'll say that. She'd be just about your age were she alive now."

"How did she die?" Maggie ventured.

"Lightning." John answered.

Maggie felt a chill ripple down her spine.

"Struck by lightning?" she asked.

"Oh, sure. You never heard about this?"

Maggie shook her head.

"Well, I'm not that surprised. Everyone in the family felt pretty bad about it. It was such an unusual death and all."

"Go on." Maggie said.

"Well, funny thing about it, as nearly as I can figure, it happened right there where the road forded Sinking Creek, right at the place we stopped the other night. I guess that gave Aunt Maura an awful scare. And then, when Lyons was almost lost..."

"What about Sarah?" Maggie persisted.

"Oh, well, this was right after they had moved to the valley. They were all full of vim and vinegar in those days. At least that's the way their letters sounded. Then we got this letter telling about Sarah's death and after that it just seemed like it broke their spirit.

"One night they were traveling home on that road, same time of year, same kinda storm. It was while Uncle Joseph was driving the horses across the ford that a bolt of lightning came down outa the sky and struck the wagon. Sarah and Annie, who were riding in the back, got hit worst. The jolt went through Sarah's body and tossed her clean out of the wagon. Happened so fast, nobody could do anything about it. The water just swept her away before anyone knew what was happening. Uncle Joseph found her body about a mile downstream the next day.

"Annie was lucky to come out alive. As it was, the lightning burnt the shoes right off her feet, scorched all the hair off her body—took three months for it to grow back. Uncle Joseph says the lightning burnt the part of her brain that makes the hearing and the talking so she's deaf and dumb to this day. It's a miracle that she's alive, way I see it. Wouldn't you say so, Maggie?"

"Yes I would," Maggie said absently. Then she turned and went inside, wanting to be off by herself for a while.

Maggie had hoped that learning about Sarah would make things better. And, in a way, it did. But Maggie felt now that the sadness of the story had begun to creep over her. Everytime she looked at Annie and saw the young girl signing with her delicate hands, she felt the tears starting in her eyes. It was just a tragedy, that was all, and no reason for it.

The gloominess Maggie felt was deepened by the harshness of the winter. Jake had been right. The winter was the most severe she had ever known. The snow piled up around the walls of the house and the wind sifted it in through the cracks between the logs so that they had to sweep the floor up several times a day, sweeping the snow out the front door into the wind. Even with both fireplaces going, they lived in a perpetual, bone-chilling cold. They wore their blanket coats inside and many times they sat down to the table wearing knitted mittens to keep their fingers from freezing while they ate. Hot food grew cold as soon as it hit the bowl. They used the chamber pot at night now, emptying it each morning so they wouldn't have to make nightly trips to the outhouse.

They passed a joyless Christmas. Mrs. McGrew forbade any festivities, although Maggie and Annie did exchange some home-made gifts in secret.

"We have no time for such frivolousness when there is so much work to be done," Mrs. McGrew had said. Actually, idleness was their greatest enemy. There was simply nothing to do. Once the meals had been prepared and the washing up was done, once wood and water had been fetched, there was nothing to do but sit in the cold and dark and wait for spring.

It was during those winter days that Maggie especially appreciated the chance to make her weekly baking trips to the cabin. Annie sometimes went with her and for the two of them it was a day out and away, up on the white snowy mountainside, away from the gloom and stillness of the house.

But Maggie especially appreciated the days when she went alone, walking in her home-made snowshoes up the mountainside, alive and awake to everything. She stoked her fires and kneaded her dough and baked the loaves with Franny on her mind. And she always returned to the mill with a new sense of strength and worth, pulling her fresh-baked bread wrapped in a blanket, lashed down on the toboggan she and Annie had made from split ash staves.

One afternoon, toward the end of the long dismal winter, Maggie was baking alone at the cabin when she heard a sound at the door. When she looked up she was surprised to see Jake Logan, dressed in his winter furs and skins. His body was covered by a huge blanket coat that trailed down to his knees. He wore a fur hat made from the entire skin of a red fox with the bushy tail trailing down his back. He took off his warm bearskin mittens and set his rifle up against the cabin wall.

"Wal, girl," he said, "I seed your smoke and figgered I'd find you here. Roust up that fire! I'm about froze. Froze for talk and bread."

Maggie smiled. "Me too. It'll be a while before the bread's ready but I can start talking anytime."

Jake settled down by the fire. "Good enough. Start talkin'."

"No, you. Tell me where you've been this winter," Maggie said.

"Wal, alright. Don't mind if I do." Jake rambled on for a good hour, telling about his solitary rambles through the mountains. He said that he had spent the worst part of the winter in a cave up along the West Branch of the Susquehanna River.

"Jest set and look at the fire, you know. Hunt a little, let the time slide by. Spend the winter drowsy and quiet like a bear, that my idee," he had said.

When Maggie brought the bread steaming from the oven they sat and had a simple meal.

"Durned if it ain't good to set and talk with you, Maggie. Man lives alone so much he fergits he has a voice, you know. Huntin's a quiet life, as a rule. Woods is that way, quiet most of the time—less there's somethin' unusual happenin'.

"But a man needs to use his voice every now and again. The same way he might feel for the handle of his knife in the dark, just to make sure it's still there. You know what I'm sayin', girl?"

Maggie nodded. Then she told Jake about her winter. When she finished the old man nodded.

"Even allowin' all the hardship and the downright weariness of it—ain't you still glad to be here?" he asked.

Maggie nodded. "Yes I am." she said truthfully.

"Wal, you know, you're not a real mountain person 'til

you've spent a winter up here. Most anybody kin pass a summer in these parts. But its the ones that lives here in the winter, those are the ones that come to know the land. And I'll tell you something else, Maggie, something the people in the valley might not understand. Once you live up in these mountains and once the feel and the roll and the rill of these hills gets in your blood, you'll never be the same again. You kin travel and ramble, as I have, but you'll never feel at home lest you're near these hills. Know what I mean Maggie?"

Maggie said she did.

"I thought so," the old man said. Then he reached into his shoulderbag and brought out a roll of thick leather. "Brought you a present," he said, "elkhide."

He spread the hide out on the floor by the hearth. "Take off them stiff boots and come over here. Put yer stockin' foot down on this leather." Maggie did as he asked and watched as he took a charred stick of wood from the fireplace and used it to trace the outline of Maggie's foot on the leather.

"I figure you been freezin' your toes long enough in them civilized shoes. Now that yer a real mountain girl, you deserve a pair of real moccasins."

Jake cut out a one-piece pattern and sat down by the fire with a deer-antler awl and a length of thread made from the twisted strands of sinew from the deer's leg.

"This is heavily-smoked elkhide," Jake said, "it'll keep your feet dry as kin be. You stuff the insides with a couple handfuls of deer hair and your feet'll be jist as toasty as kin be, no matter what the weather is."

Jake felt like talking.

"Used to know an old Susquehannock Indian woman,

her name in English would be 'Small Stitches', or some-thin' like that. She was give that name because, even in old age, she was skillful with an awl or needle. Why she could sew up anything. Made me a set of buckskins once when I was a young man.

"'Small Stitches' said one time that you can tell an awful lot about people by just lookin' at what they wears on their feet. She pointed out that most white folks wear them heavy shoes with thick soles and high heels on 'em. Can't even feel the ground under their feet—fergit they're walkin' on the earth.

"She said that was why the white folks were so funny about land. Always wantin' to buy and sell it and trade it back and forth. Almost like they weren't part of it—like it wasn't a part of 'em in some way, you know what I'm sayin' girl?"

Maggie nodded.

"Well, that's the good thing about moccasins, you feel connected to the ground when you wear these—like a tree has roots, you see what I mean?"

Maggie smiled.

Jake slipped the finished moccasins on her feet. Maggie admired them in the firelight. They were made from one piece of leather, with a puckered toe and a seam down the center and long cuffs that could be folded up and tied around the ankle to keep the snow out.

"Thank you for this present, Jake. I thank you and my feet thank you." Then Maggie stopped short. "But how am I goin' to explain where these came from when I get down to the mill tonight?"

Jake smiled. "You could tell the truth."

Maggie shook her head. "But that would place you in danger. If McGrew knew you visited me here, he might try to set a trap for you."

Jake nodded. "That's true, girl. That's true. Well, you could always tell them you took them offen a dead Indian. That would gladden their dark hearts."

Maggie frowned. "Their hearts aren't too dark."

"They're killin' off the wild things, Maggie. I don't know anything darker than that. They're chasin' the game out of the valley, fishin' out the streams, cloudin' up the skies with their chimbly smoke."

"I think you're making too much of it." she said. "After all, there are only 17 families in this valley. There's plenty of room for everyone."

"Seventeen too many if you ask me. That's the beginning of civilization, girl. Ya know what that means to me? That means a man could get arrested and throwed in chains for doin' what comes natural. Can't think of anything that comes darker than that."

Then the old man smiled. "But yer doin' right girl. Keep bakin' that bread."

Maggie sighed. "The McGrew's aren't bad people. It's mostly Mrs. McGrew that rubs me wrong. She's so sorrowful all the time. A woman like that can drag a body down. I don't really feel like I own my own life. I'm still bound-out to her."

Maggie glanced around the cabin. "Ya know, when spring comes, I think I'll give this place a real good cleaning. Maybe get some tables and chairs in here so we have something besides the ground to sit on."

The old man smiled, knowing what she was thinking. "You'll have to get the roof fixed for the spring rains," he said. "And then o'course you'll have to put in a good size garden."

Maggie looked at the old man. "Jake, I sometimes get the feeling that this is my real home up here, up in this cabin. Know what I mean?"

The old man nodded. "Girl, I have a feelin' that as long as you keep bakin' that bread, you'll never want for anything in this valley. You're a real mountain girl now, Maggie, free to do as you will. No need to be bound-out anymore."

That afternoon, when the old man left, Maggie sent him away with two loaves of bread: one in his stomach and one in his shoulderbag.

Maggie walked back down to the mill that night, delighting in the warmth of her new moccasins. It felt good to feel the earth under her feet. By the time she reached the house, she had made her decision.

When Maggie came into the house, Mrs. McGrew's eyes instantly went to Maggie's feet. But the older woman said nothing.

It was Joseph McGrew who noticed them when they sat down to dinner that night.

"Maggie," he said, "what are those on your feet?"

Maggie took a deep breath. "Indian moccasins."

"Where did you get them?"

"I traded for them."

"Maggie, you haven't been dealing with the Indians, have you?"

Maggie said nothing.

"I will not have anyone in this house who conspires with the heathens. Do you hear?"

"Just as well," Maggie said, "because I don't plan to be a member of this household for much longer." She was surprised at how strong and firm her voice sounded.

"I have decided that when the spring comes, I'm goin' to move up to Franny's cabin."

"Why, Maura, do you hear this? Our bound-out girl is

talking of leaving us. No child. That cannot be. After all, we have an agreement."

"That's right," Maggie said, "the agreement was that I would work for my keep here until I could return to Philadelphia. I don't see anyone anxious to have me go. And I don't have a home there anyway. But can't you see? I could make a home for myself up there on the mountainside."

McGrew laughed. "But Maggie, this is preposterous. How will you get your living?"

"I'll bake bread and trade for what I need, just as Franny did. This valley needs a proper Bread Sister again."

"But Maggie, you're just a child."

Maggie's eyes blazed with anger. "A child couldn't work as I have in this household! Haven't I chopped and hauled and cooked and washed? Haven't I done a woman's work in this house? Done everything but bear children here?"

"Maura," McGrew said, "speak to her, bring her to reason."

Mrs. McGrew looked across the room. Her eyes met Maggie's.

"Let her go," Mrs. McGrew said.

McGrew looked confused. "But, Maura, this is preposterous. We can't afford to lose her labor here and surely you don't believe this is in her best interests."

"I said: Let her go. She won't starve up there, I'll wager that. And there's nothing to be gained by holdin' her."

McGrew brought his fist down on the table. "I am the head of this family!" he shouted.

"And I am the head of this household," Mrs. McGrew returned. "I said: Let her go."

Knowing he was defeated, McGrew's anger suddenly vanished.

"I mean you no harm, Maggie," he said amiably. "It's not just our own self-interest, but your safety I fear for. We have come to grow quite fond of you here."

"It would grieve us deeply if you came to some harm at the hands of the savages. I beseech you: Avoid the Indians at all costs. They are not human as we are and know nothing of goodness or mercy."

McGrew suddenly became very interested in the food on his plate. "I'll be glad when the spring comes and we don't have to eat this parched corn anymore," he said.

The spring did come. And just as Maggie had willed, she moved her few possessions up to Franny's cabin and began to make herself a home.

Her first evening alone in the cabin she made herself a simple supper and ate it sitting in the open air on her

doorstep.

An early moon rose up yellow and full above the mountains. It was a warm April night. Maggie decided to enjoy her new freedom by taking a moonlit walk. She walked to the edge of the clearing and found a deerpath, leading her up the mountainside. She walked quietly, feeling the ground under her moccasins. There were still patches of snow in sheltered places in the woods but the wind blew warm, carrying the promise of spring. She followed the path to the top of the mountain. This was the first of the seven mountain ranges and was called First Mountain.

She gazed down at the valley below. It seemed so quiet and serene. Here and there she could see plumes of chimney smoke rising from points on the moonlit landscape.

Then she turned her face west, towards the mountains. The wind blew, kicking her red hair out in the breeze. She could feel its force pushing against her body. She looked westward, out over the seven mountain ranges and saw those ridges rolling across the horizon like dark, hump-backed snakes. She knew that somewhere out there, towards the Ohio valley, Franny was still alive, plowing and planting and baking bread. And that thought was a tremendous comfort to her.

Chapter Eight

Maggie's first summer in the wilderness passed like all summers in the mountains: gloriously. And quickly. The summer had a funny way of ending before Maggie was ready. When the first cool days of the fall came on, it was almost as though there really hadn't been any summer at all. It was almost as though the whole season was little more than a half-remembered dream.

It was an important summer for Maggie. Settled in Franny's cabin, she didn't feel bound-out anymore. She felt like she was becoming her own woman. She became The Bread Sister, just like Franny before her.

And just as they had done with her aunt, the settlement women traded for the bread and came to Maggie's door whenever they needed a warm welcoming ear. There were troubles aplenty on the frontier and Maggie got to hear all of them. In that way she became a friend to women many years older than her. She gained a special trust, the kind a Bread Sister should have. Maggie began to see that there was a great deal more to being The Bread Sister than simply baking bread. It had to do with a way of giving that Maggie was only beginning to understand.

That fall was an extra busy one in the valley. The crops came in good and folks scurried to get things stowed away for the long mountain winter.

It was going to be a cold one that year. Everybody said so. Jake even mentioned it when he visited Maggie's cabin that fall.

"The signs is clear, girl," he said. "Hairs are long on the caterpillar and squirrels are diggin' deep. Means we're in for a real mean winter, mark my words."

They talked until late. Then Jake rolled up in his woolen blanket by the fire and Maggie retired to her rope mattress bed, wrapped warm in her turkey feather quilt. The next morning at breakfast, she said, "Jake, I had a dream about you last night."

The old man scratched his headful of hair. "Always interested in dreams, girl. Tell me about it."

Maggie wrinkled her brow, straining to remember all the details.

"I saw you walking through the woods, in a terrible deep snow, so deep you sunk in right up to your thighs. You were looking for me. I was lost but somehow I couldn't call out to you. I think I was in a deep dark sleep.

"Then you saw a herd of deer, you raised your rifle to fire, thinking to collect us some meat, but before you could pull the trigger, something strange happened. The deer started to point with their noses, all of 'em, pointing as though they were trying to tell you something. As though they were trying to say 'She's this-away, she's this-away.'" Maggie paused.

"Well," said Jake impatiently, "what happened then?"

Maggie shook her head. "I don't know. The dream ended."

Jake scratched his head again.

"Well, now that's a puzzle," he said. "Ya know, the Indians set great store by their dreams. Now you take a fella like Old Hammerstone, he's an old Lenape holy man. Why, he'd sit up all night with a dream like that. He'd smoke and ponder on it. And come morning, he would read that dream for ya, revealin' its true meanin'."

Maggie handed Jake a steaming cup of spearmint tea.

"Do you believe in reading dreams?" she asked.

The old man nodded. "Well, sure. I s'pose. Up to a point, that is. But ya know them Indians, they carry it too far. They read meanin' inta everything: rocks, trees, animals, plants, wind and water. I even seed those old timers set up at night, readin' inta the stars. Now that's too many for me. Me, I'll stick to hairs on the caterpillar and squirrels diggin' deep. Those are signs a body can depend on."

The old man was right about the weather. The snow started falling the day after he left and kept right on

falling, thick and steady, for two days. The mountains were covered with a fresh white mantle of snow. Leafless trees stood out stark and black against the whiteness of the mountainsides. The small streams froze solid. Sinking Creek became clogged with snow and ice. Then the winds came and began pushing the snow around, piling it into drifts which, in the hollows, were as tall as a man. The wind howled for days after the snow stopped falling.

Sometimes at night, during the snowstorms, Maggie felt as though she was riding in the cabin of a sailing ship, plunging through a raging storm at sea.

But she was safe and snug. She had plenty of firewood piled by the door. She snapped off the icicles that froze to the eaves and melted them down for water. She had stores of provisions—dried herbs and kegs of flour and pots of honey and strings of dried apples. She had a sense of great wealth and security.

On these snowbound days, as a special gift to the people in the valley, Maggie baked up fifty loaves of holiday breads. The dough was formed into twirls and topped with dried apples and cherries. Some loaves came out of the oven looking lop-sided and funny. But others were masterpieces.

The day before Christmas, the weather grew calm and cleared. Maggie decided to bundle up the bread and take it down to the mill to give out to the neighbors when they came by on their regular rounds. She planned to stay Christmas Eve with the McGrew's, as she had for the last several years, then return late on Christmas day.

Traveling on these winter days, Maggie found that it was easiest to transport the bread on a toboggan she and Annie had made from split wooden ash staves. The toboggan was long and narrow so it would pass easily down the trail: Nine feet long and a little less than a foot wide. In front, the staves were bent up into a graceful curve, like the front of a horse-drawn sleigh. Maggie lashed the bread bundle down with a long piece of rope.

It was just while she was completing the lashings that she saw Annie toiling up the mountain trail, clomping along in her snowshoes. Like Maggie, she was dressed warmly: a thick woolen blanket coat, layers and layers of warm stockings, thick boots and a knitted cap and mittens.

"Merry Christmas!" Maggie shouted. Her breath made clouds in the air.

Annie took off her mittens so she could sign properly.

"Some storm," Annie signed, "It's good to be outside. Are you headed down to the house?" Maggie nodded.

"Good," Annie signed. "Because Papa sent me to fetch you. We're having a big gathering at the house tonight and

Papa said you're to come and bring some bread."

"The old goat thinks of everything," Maggie said. "But I thought your mother disapproved of parties."

Annie laughed. "Papa talked her into it this year. He says it's important for his political career, to have everyone in the valley over for a party. He's going to make a speech."

Maggie smiled. "I wouldn't miss that for anything," she said. "I hope your mother isn't too upset by all the festivities."

"The storm helped a lot," Annie signed, "Mama got so stir crazy from being inside that she even got out needle and thread and helped Lyons and I string popcorn chains for decorations."

Maggie was hungry for sociability after her days of solitude at the cabin. "Let's go!" she shouted.

They started down the mountain trail. Annie walked ahead, breaking the trail with her snowshoes, Maggie walked behind in her own snowshoes, dragging the toboggan behind her. It slid easily over the packed snow. Because the snowshoes were so clumsy to walk in, both girls carried walking sticks to help keep their balance.

About halfway down the mountainside, well into the thick hemlocks, where the trail shot steeply downhill, Annie stopped. She turned around on the trail and removed her mittens. Maggie knew she had something to say.

Annie's hands moved gracefully through the cold air.

"This is too slow," she signed. "I'm anxious to get there. Let's just hop in this thing and ride down to the mill. We'd be there in no time."

Maggie had never attempted the mountain trail on the toboggan but she saw the sense in what Annie had said. It was a fairly straight shot down to the flatlands, she reasoned. They could probably take the turns alright and if they got going too fast, all they had to do was put out their feet and stop themselves.

Maggie made the sign for "I agree," and they knelt and began unlashing the bundle so they could shift it back in the bed of the toboggan, making room for them to sit in front, directly behind the bow. They lashed down their walking sticks and snowshoes. Maggie seated herself in front and Annie pushed them off and jumped on behind, locking her arms around Maggie's waist.

It was amazing how quickly the toboggan picked up speed. The girls hurtled down the mountainside, the wind tearing at their clothes and hair.

Then it happened. Maggie didn't even see the half-buried log lying in the center of the trail. Even if she would have, there wouldn't have been a way to avoid hitting it.

The bow of the toboggan glanced off the log and sent them flying off the trail, careening down through the woods. They whipped through a blackberry thicket. The branches stung their faces as they flew past and kept right on going. Trees flashed by in a blur. Maggie felt Annie clinging to her waist in sheer terror.

For a moment they were headed directly for a huge hemlock tree which would have smashed them to splinters. But somehow they managed to lean to the side and veer the toboggan away at the last moment.

Then Maggie saw it coming up: a deep sinkhole filled with boulders and drifted snow. Before Maggie could put out her legs to stop, the toboggan shot out over the lip of the sinkhole and dropped like a rock.

It seemed as though they fell in slow motion. The toboggan dropped away from them and Maggie caught a glimpse of it flipping end-for-end, down into the sinkhole. The lashings came loose and the blanket flew open, scattering the bread out across the snow, all round the lip of the depression. The toboggan struck a piece of rock that jutted out from the snow and stopped dead on its side.

Maggie and Annie hit the snow, came down hard and kept rolling. Maggie put her arms out to stop herself but then realized that the snow underneath them was sliding as well. They had created a tiny avalanche that pushed them down further into the hole. Annie came pinwheeling along and, quite by accident, the girls collided. Annie's heavy boot heel swung around and caught Maggie on the forehead, just above the left eye. After that, Maggie didn't feel much.

Maggie had no way of knowing how long she laid there

in the deep snow. When she came to her senses, everything was quiet and dark and still. She couldn't hear the wind. All she heard was her own breathing.

Then she tried to move. She was startled to find that she couldn't. She willed her arms and legs to move. But they wouldn't. She thought they must be broken. She felt a terrible weight resting on her back, holding her, face down, in the snow. Then a thought leaped into her mind that sent a shiver of panic through her whole body. She must be buried. Buried alive in the drifted snow at the bottom of the sinkhole.

Straining every muscle in her upper body, she managed to turn her head to the side. She could tell by the feel of the snow against her face that her breath had melted a small cave around her head. It was in rolling her head around that her cheek struck something fuzzy. It was her hand, covered by a frozen woolen mitten. She realized that she must have fallen with her arm underneath her and her right hand close to her face. She worked her fingers inside the frozen mitt. They tingled painfully as the blood began to quicken in them.

She began working her hand back and forth, inching it forward like an underground animal, burrowing a hole through the snow. She moved it ahead a few inches and was eventually able to punch her way up into the breath cave, which had increased in size, due to her exertions. Using her right hand, she could push the snow around a little, pushing it back against the chamber walls, making the space even larger. The space was now the size of a bushel basket but only her arm and head were free.

Then she struck something hard. As she poked at it, it frightened her by wiggling. It must be Annie's hand, she thought.

They gripped hands. At least Annie was still alive.

Maggie rested, her face laying in the snow, her breath coming in tortured gasps. It was exhausting to work in this position. Annie squeezed her friend's hand encouragingly. Even through the frozen mitten, Maggie felt Annie's friendship, urging her on.

They lay there for what seemed like hours. Then Maggie got the strength to thrash around with her right arm. She struck something in the roof of her breath cave. She reached up and closed her mittened hand around it. It was one of their walking sticks. Somehow it had landed in the layer of snow above them.

Maggie grabbed the tip of the stick and pulled it down into the cave then thrust it up. She felt some resistance for a few feet then felt the top of the stick break through the surface of the snow above them. She quickly calculated. The walking sticks were five feet long. That meant they must be buried under at least four feet of snow. All hopes of digging their way out vanished. They were trapped.

Maggie thrust the stick up at the roof of the cave. Snow poured down the hole, covering her head, but she kept thrusting, then ringed the stick round and round until she had made a hole about three inches across. A weak shower of light fell down through the hole, along with a draft of fresh, clean air. Maggie pushed the pole up as far as she could get it and lodged it there. Then she rested.

She must have fallen asleep because the next thing she knew, Annie was wringing her hand and startling her awake. They were both aware of the danger of drifting off to sleep in their situation. They both knew that that was the way people froze to death, by laying in the cold and allowing themselves to give in to the drowsiness that is the first sign of the freezing death. Annie knew this well and she had the sense that Maggie had worked very hard and was very tired and would drop off to sleep very easily. So Annie vigilantly wrung Maggie's hand whenever the grip went limp.

Maggie's mind started to drift. She went in and out of consciousness. At times she didn't care anymore. She just wanted to be allowed to sleep. She was furious with Annie for gripping her hand so tightly. She tried to pull away but Annie held her firm by the mitten. The anger was good

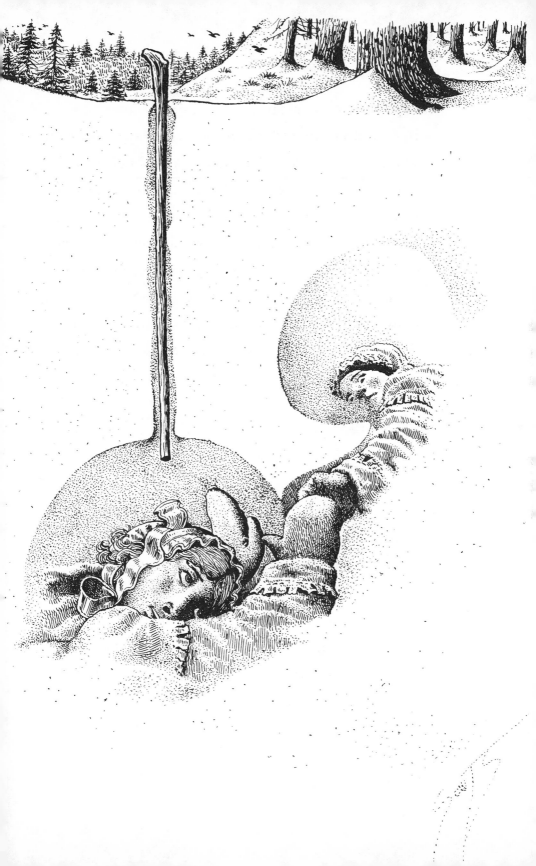

because it kept her awake.

In one of her more lucid moments, Maggie began to calculate their chances. She knew they probably wouldn't be missed at the house until nightfall. If the folks at the mill came out to find them, would they be able to see the toboggan trail in the dark? And would they know where to dig even if they found the toboggan lying on its side in the sinkhole? Maggie also knew that all this would have to happen tonight. They couldn't wait until the light of morning. She knew the two of them would never survive the night in the terrible, bone-chilling cold.

Maggie felt as though her body was already dead. The fingers of her right hand felt frozen, gripped in Annie's mitten. Her mind began to fade in and out.

She felt as though she were hanging on the edge of sleep. Like she were hanging on the edge of a high cliff, waiting to fall and wanting to fall. The only question was when she should tell herself to stop hanging on.

Maggie lay awake like that for hours. It grew darker. She was half-awake half-asleep, waiting out the terrible cold and fighting off the almost irresistible urge to close her eyes and drift off into what she thought would be the softest and most comfortable sleep she had ever known.

Chapter Nine

Jake felt like a fool for traveling in this weather. But he knew if he kept pushing, he would make Maggie's cabin by nightfall.

He felt a powerful urge to visit Maggie on this Christmas Eve. She was a link with the human world. And he cherished that link.

Just as the sun was dipping down, Jake broke out into the clearing. He smiled as he remembered how Maggie had looked that first day she had come into the valley. He had walked right up behind her that day. He wouldn't be able to do that now, he thought. Her ears had gotten sharper. And he had gotten older.

It was strange, he thought, to get old in a land he thought would always be young and full of life. He once heard an old hunter say that it was never the mountains that quit a man, it was always the other way around. He thought maybe he was beginning to understand what that old-timer had meant.

Jake opened the door and hollered inside. No answer. He crept around in the darkness. The hearthfire coals were still warm. Her snowshoes were gone. Then he remembered that she usually spent Christmas Eve at the mill. He had forgotten about that. Well, he thought, he'd just build up the fire and wait for her and welcome her when she returned the next day.

Jake went back outside to bring in a load of firewood. Then he saw them: a herd of white-tail deer, picking their way down the trail. Strange for them to travel in such deep snow, he thought. They usually stayed holed up somewhere in deep snow like this. Then he saw that the toboggan had packed the snow into an easily traveled trail. They must be taking advantage of the path to forage for food.

Which reminded him, his meat bag was empty. Wouldn't it be fine to shoot Maggie a nice fat doe and present it to her when she returned the next day? And couldn't he use a taste of fresh venison hump tonight? He went back inside for his rifle which he had left leaning against the cabin wall.

He checked his rifle in the dimming light. There was already powder and a ball in the barrel. He opened the flashpan and poured in a spot of gunpowder from his priming horn, then snapped the frizzen shut. He was ready. And he had better move fast. The light was failing.

He crept down the trail. All his senses were alive. The wind was to his face so they wouldn't scent him. He would follow the deer quietly, then circle around and take his shot while there was still a glimmer of light on the horizon.

The deer were stepping right in the toboggan tracks. That made the tracking easy, even in the failing light.

Then he saw them, herded up around the lip of the sinkhole, sniffing and pawing at the snow and pointing with their noses. He raised his rifle to shoot, centering in on a large doe poised on the edge of the snowy precipice.

Then Maggie's dream flashed into the old man's mind. He lowered his rifle and took another look at the deer. They were acting peculiar, as though they were trying to get at something down in that hole. Moving silently, Jake crept up to the hole on hands and knees. At last the doe winded him and snorted and bounded away. But he didn't care about that now. He wanted to see what was down in that hole. Near the edge of the sinkhole he found a loaf of bread that had been nibbled on.

Then, down among the boulders and drifted snow, he

picked out other loaves, strewn out across the whiteness. Then he saw the smashed toboggan, lying on its side in the drift. All at once the picture came together in his head.

He slid down the snowy incline and found the nub of the walking stick jutting up through the snow. He began digging furiously with his mittens. The first thing he saw was Maggie's head, her hair frozen to the snow. Using his mittens like twin shovels, he dug her out. Her face was blue with cold. He scraped back most of the snow but when he tried to lift her out he saw that her hand was frozen to something.

It was then that he discovered Annie's hand and realized that she was buried as well. Quickly, he swept the snow back from Annie's dark form.

All the while he was digging, his mind was working furiously. He considered the things he could do. He could gather wood and strike up a fire. But that would take time and he didn't know if he could thaw them there in the open. No, he would have to get them in out of the weather.

He considered strapping them to the toboggan and pulling them up to the cabin. But that would take even longer.

Then he realized what he must do. He would have to go downhill, down to the mill. It would be fast and sure and even though he knew McGrew might make trouble for him when he got there, he realized it was the girls' best chance.

Jake wrapped the girls in the blanket and lashed their bodies to the toboggan. He checked their breathing by placing his ear down close to their lips. They were still alive, sure enough, but Jake knew they were in that deep frozen sleep that comes before the white death.

With his rifle in one hand and the toboggan drag-rope in the other, he heaved them up out of the sinkhole and backtracked to the mountain trail. Jake skidded them downhill fast, trotting along through the deep snow to keep up. When he reached the mill, he was surprised to see that the yard was a mass of sleighs and horses. Inside he could hear the laughter and shouting of dozens of people.

He kicked the door open and dashed into the house, pulling the snow-covered toboggan right across the wooden floor and up to the blazing hearthfire.

The guests, seated at the table and lounging around the fire, gasped in terror. John, who had been standing near the door, moved to bar Jake's way. "What's the meaning of this?" he demanded.

Moving forward like an old bear, Jake swung one of his huge mittened hands and knocked the young man out of the way, sending him sprawling out across the floor.

The wind howled in through the open door. Jake knelt and threw back the blanket that covered the girls' faces. They lay like two corpses, half-covered with ice and snow.

Someone in the back of the room started wailing. It was Mrs. McGrew. She broke through the crowd and fell on her knees by the toboggan.

"They're dead!" she screamed, "dead and gone!"

The old man shook his head. "No they ain't. Now

lookee here, gimme yer hand." He took Mrs. McGrew's hand and placed it by Annie's lips so she could feel the shallow breathing that still ebbed and flowed within her.

Jake turned around and looked at the rest of the people. They stood wide-eyed and stunned by what they saw.

The old man's voice cracked like a whip. "No time fer standin' and starin' now! There's still a trickle o' life left in these two and we kin bring 'em back if we move smart now! Git that door closed! Some o' you men, get that fire rousted up! You women bring kettles o' coldish water over here to bath 'em in! Move, now!"

Jake's voice galvanized the crowd into action. People began scurrying about like ants. McGrew brought out an enormous set of bellows and began building up the fire. Some women knelt down by the girls and began to cut the frozen clothing off their bodies with bread knives and sewing scissors.

Once the girls were wrapped in warm blankets by the fire, Jake coached the women on how to soak the girls' feet and hands in lukewarm water and warm them up slow.

When their frost-bitten toes and ears and fingers began to thaw, Maggie and Annie came out of their sleep and began howling in pain.

Maggie, wild-eyed, grabbed Jake's sleeve and drew him down to her.

"Can't ya make it stop, Jake? The pain's somethin' awful."

The old man nodded. "I know, girl, I know. Froze a couple toes in my time, that I have. But you should be glad girl. Be glad yer alive to feel the pain."

Maggie nodded, her eyes closed. "I know, Jake, I know. It was only luck that you found us."

The old man chuckled. "No, Maggie, weren't no luck in it. It was yer dream. Them deer led me right to ya."

Maggie didn't understand that. And her mind was too clouded with pain for her to care. But she realized that Jake was right. She should feel lucky to feel the pain, her and Annie. They should feel lucky to be alive.

Jake stood up and glanced at the front door of the McGrew's house, bolted against the cold weather. It was a dozen steps away. If he moved quickly through the confusion, he thought he might be able to slip out the door and make his get-away.

"Christmas night," he said to himself, "and they'd love to celebrate by roasting a heathen like me over the fire."

People had begun to celebrate now, raising their glasses and shouting, doubly merry because the girls were safe and sound. Across the room, Jake saw McGrew watching him. The big man sat down his tankard of cider and shouldered his way through the crowd. Jake prepared himself to fight his way out if need be.

McGrew stood facing the old man. "I saw your eyes reaching for the door," McGrew said. Then he smiled broadly and extended his hand.

"I wouldn't turn a dog out on a night like this," McGrew said. "You saved my little girl's life and Maggie's too. You can't be all that much of a heathen to have done that. Stay and be our guest this evening. After all, it's Christmas."

Mrs. McGrew came and took Jake by the arm. "I've set a place for you at the table. Come and sit."

The heavy plank table was loaded with a savory feast: roast goose with wild grape sauce, sweet potatoes, corn cakes, broiled venison and hot onion soup. It was enough to make the old man's mouth water.

People settled down and sat.

"Let us pray," McGrew said. "We are thankful," he began, "for the goodness and bounty of our lives as well as the miraculous rescue of our girls from the jaws of the white and frigid death. And Lord, we are especially blessed to have with us tonight a man, Jacob Logan, a buckskinned angel of the frontier. Guide him in your ways and help him to see the light. In the Lord's name, Amen."

The "Amens" went around the table and were drowned out by the clatter of forks and tinware. All these miracles had brought on a terrific hunger.

They feasted. Then they settled into that lazy, comfortable feeling that well-fed people have when the fire burns low and its good to sit and smoke and listen to stories by the hearthfire.

Both men and women settled themselves, close back in the shadows. Mrs. McGrew blew out the candles so they had only the light from the fire.

The stage was set. McGrew seized the opportunity to display his oratorical skills.

"Now some people say," he began, "that this has been a cold winter."

People nodded in agreement.

"But friends and neighbors: cold? You call this cold? I have seen some cold weather in my time that would make this winter seem like a day in July. Now you take the winter of 1771—that was a cold winter."

"How cold was it?" someone asked.

"Well, I can't tell you in scientific terms, but I will say this. One frigid morning, I was walking out to the mill, whistling as I went. But I noticed that no sound came from my lips. I looked up in the air and I can hardly describe my surprise at what I saw. It was so cold that day that those musical notes had just frozen solid in the air. Hung there like icicles.

"So I reached up and plucked them out of the air, put them in my pocket and went about my work. At the end of the day I came back in the house and laid those musical notes out on the hearth to thaw. We sat at the table and heard a little whistle escape as each one thawed.

"Well that gave me an idea. I went out the next day and whistled all day while I stacked bags of grain at the mill. Came in that night and laid those musical notes I collected out on the hearth, laid them all out in order. And we sat there that evening and listened to what must have been about an hour of really nice music."

Laughter filled the room. A few others told their own stories, recounting cold winters past.

Then McGrew's eyes fell on Jake, who had been sitting quietly, listening.

"Tell us, Mr. Logan," he said, "surely you must have some tale of a cold winter. Perhaps a daring hunting exploit or possibly an account of some escape from savage Indians that might delight us."

All eyes fell on Jake. He took a long time in answering.

"Well, it's true," the old man began, "I s'pose I have seen some cold winters up in these mountains. I 'member one year I was huntin' bear over on the second ridge.

Managed to roust one right out of his hibernation spot too. He was madder'n a hornet. So he starts for me, with blood in his eye."

Jake rose from his seat, hooking his arms up like the bear's, extending his fingers like sharp claws.

"So I raised my rifle and was just about to pull the trigger when I realized that I had done about the stupidest things you can imagine."

"What was that?" someone asked.

"Well," Jake answered, "I'd poured powder down the barrel and I'd primed the flashpan but I had forgotten to cram a ball down the barrel. So there I stood with an unloaded gun, bear chargin' down on me."

"What'd you do?" somebody asked.

"Well, nothin' I could do. That bear had me backed up against a rock cliff and I'll tell you, I was plenty scared. Got so scared, the sweat started ta run down my forehead.

"But it was so cold that day that those little drops o' sweat froze hard inta little balls o' ice. I reached up to wipe the sweat away and I felt those iceballs and I got an idee!

"I plucked one of those iceballs off my forehead and rammed it down the barrel of my gun. Just in time too, because that bear had reared up on his hind legs and was about to pounce on me. I raised my rifle and fired. The shot went off just fine. But the heat from the exploding

powder melted that iceball and there wasn't anything but a big splatter o' water goin' through the air toward that bear.

"Fortunately, it was so cold that day that that water re-froze into a sharp icicle. And that icicle went in right between the bear's eyes.

"But that bear's body heat was so fierce, it just melted that icicle . . . and that pore old bear died of water on the brain."

People collapsed in laughter. There was no end to the laughing. It just went on like that all night. Then somebody brought out a fiddle and they cleared back the furniture and began to dance. Jake even got up and danced a reel with the widow Brown from down on Penn's Creek.

Maggie and Annie watched it all from their blankets by the fire. They felt weak and their hands and feet still pained them. But there was so much joy in the house that night, a person just couldn't let little aches and pains draw off any of the fun.

Annie touched Maggie on the shoulder. "Close your eyes," she signed. She placed a present, wrapped in paper, in the older girl's lap. "For Christmas, for you."

Maggie unwrapped it and drew out a finely made basket of woven ash splints. "Thank you, Annie. It's a real gift, sure. Yer so clever with your hands." Then Maggie thought about the bread loaves strewn out across the snow.

"But I don't have anything for you," she said. "Or for anyone else here. I had made the bread all special. I made you a special loaf with your name writ right in the dough."

Annie shook her head and began signing. "Don't worry," her hands said, "you give your gift all year long. But there is something you could give me. Something more precious than a single loaf of bread."

"Say it, Annie, and it's yours."

"Will you teach me to bake the Callahan Bread? I've been meaning to ask you for a long time."

Maggie didn't have to take time to consider. She knew it was the right thing to do.

"It'll be a privilege, Annie, passin' the bread bakin' on to the likes of you. You've got my promise on it then— you'll know the bread bakin' secrets."

Annie grinned broad then rolled over and fell asleep by the fire.

Maggie saw Mrs. McGrew coming to her, through the crowd.

"Maggie," she said, "I have something to say to you and I don't know exactly how to say it."

Maggie sat with an open ear.

"Something broke loose in me tonight, Maggie, something that's been tight and held for years now. When Mr. Logan threw back that blanket and I saw you two laying there, I knew you were dead. I just knew it. And I realized in that moment that I loved you every bit as much as I loved my own little Annie."

She began to cry. "You see, I had a daughter once—"

Maggie put a hand on her shoulder. "I know." she said softly.

"You know about Sarah?"

Maggie nodded.

"And how she died?"

Maggie nodded again.

"Well, after she was buried, I thought I would just go on, you know, but I never could be the same. I carried that grief around like a stone on my back.

"Then you came along. From the first moment I saw you, all I could see was my Sarah standing there—she'd be just about your age, you know. And it hurt, it just twisted the knife in the wound. So it was torture to be near you. But I couldn't send you away, understand?"

Maggie nodded, tears coming into her eyes.

"Then tonight, when I saw you laying there, I realized that it was too late. It was too late to do anything about any of it, because you were gone and dead. But you're not dead . . ."

"No." Maggie laughed.

"And it's not too late. Life is hard, Maggie, but it's not as hard as I've made it. And so what if it is hard?

"We're alive, Maggie. We're all alive and we're together. And you know what? It's Christmas, Maggie! It's really Christmas!"

Maggie nodded and they embraced for a long moment by the fire. Then Mrs. McGrew eased Maggie down by the fire where she could sleep and pulled up her blanket.

Maggie laid back, eyes closed, feeling the warmth of the fire on her face. She smiled. Someone was playing the fiddle, soft. Just before she drifted off to sleep, she heard the sound of people singing. Rising above the music was one voice—beautiful and clear like a bell, like the voice of someone who had sung on the stage. Maggie didn't have to open her eyes to know who it was.

Chapter Ten

In the winter days that followed, Maggie kept her promise to Annie. She taught Annie the bread-baking secrets just as Franny had taught her, years ago in Philadelphia. Even though Annie wasn't a real Callahan, she took to the bread baking just fine. She was soon able to bake up rounded golden loaves on her own, using the spook yeast from Maggie's pouch.

In passing on the mysteries of the bread baking, it occurred to Maggie that she had become a link in a long, loving chain of women who had passed the bread baking along, year after year, keeping the spook yeast going.

Spring came on. Down in the marshlands along Sinking Creek, Maggie could see the vivid green shoots of the skunk cabbage pushing their way up through the snow that still lay on the ground. She knew the long weary winter was over.

On a warm April evening, Maggie had taken a packbasket of loaves down to the mill. She left the loaves with Annie and had supper with the McGrews.

After the washing up was done, Maggie shouldered her empty packbasket and started for home by the moonlight. The moon had risen up full above the mountains, bathing everything in a ghostly, dreamy light.

When Maggie came to the millpond, she saw the moon reflected up in the water and she was so pulled by its beauty that she sat down in the tall grass on the pondbank to admire it. She saw the moon above, hanging white and lovely in the sky. And the moon below, reflected on the rippled surface of the pond.

"Two moons." She said to herself. She liked the sound of the words so she said them again, out loud: "Two moons."

Then she heard a noise behind her. Someone was walking through the tall grass towards her. She turned and could make out John, coming across the clearing, walking lazy with his hands in his pockets. The moonlight picked up the white of his shirt and the dark bars of the suspenders that held up his pants.

He walked up beside her.

"Mind if I set with you?" he asked.

Maggie sat with her back straight.

"It's a free country," Maggie said, "set where ya will."

"Alright, don't mind if I do."

He had scarcely settled himself before he started talking.

"You know, Maggie, sometimes I come out here and set just like this—just set and look at that ol' moon hangin' up there in the sky. Sure is pretty, don't you think?"

Maggie turned her face up to the moon. "Surely is," she said.

"And I look out across this ground," John continued. "Pretty piece of ground, wouldn't you say?"

Maggie nodded. "Yes I would."

John forged ahead. "Now you take that rise over there, just before you get to the edge of the clearing. I've often said to myself that would make a good spot for a house, good place for a young couple to settle and get a start in life. Don't you think so, Maggie?"

Maggie looked the ground over. "Well," she said at last, "I suppose it would be alright. Awful close to neighbors, though."

"Well," John chuckled, "that's all in how you look at it. They wouldn't be just neighbors. They'd be family." John paused a moment to let the gravity of the suggestion sink in, "That is, if your name happened to be McGrew. Do you catch my drift, Maggie?"

"No, I don't." she said.

"Well, let me put it to you just as plain as I can. What I'm talking about is marriage. Look, Maggie, let's quit beating about the bush: It's been on my mind and I know it's been on your mind and, well, everybody's talking about it. Everybody knows that marriage is the next step for me and you."

Maggie's eyes flashed with anger. "You? Why, I'd no more marry you than the man in the moon. And even if I did want to get married, we're not even the same age. You're way too old for me."

John laughed. "No, Maggie, not at all. I'm only three years ahead of you and besides, it's natural that the man should be older."

"What's natural about that?"

"Well, I don't know. Just makes sense, I guess. I suppose the Lord made it that way so that wives could ask their husband's advice when they get confused about something."

"Advice?" Maggie laughed. "John, I don't mean to hurt your feelings but you don't even have the sense to lead a church meeting in silent prayer, let alone give advice. You'd do best to stick to your millwork."

Undaunted, John turned his reasonable side. "Now listen, Maggie, you can't stay up on that mountainside forever. Time'll come when you'll come down into the valley and start a family and take your place in the community."

"I got a place," Maggie said, standing up. "And this conversation gets ridiculous. I'm headed home." She reached down for her packbasket.

John took her by the shoulders and spun her around to face him.

"You're a good girl now, Maggie. You'll see the sense of it. You'll come around to my way of thinking. Especially after this—" and he drew her to him, his lips searching for hers in the moonlight.

Maggie felt a powerful rage boiling up inside her. She grabbed him by the suspenders, swung him around three times and let him fly. John took two dizzy steps backwards and fell head over heels into the millpond. A moment later, he surfaced, sputtering and hollering at the top of his lungs.

"Maggie," he shouted, "Git me out of here. I can't swim!" He thrashed about like a drowning man.

Maggie grabbed her knees and threw her head back and laughed. "I should've guessed that," she said. She felt around on the ground and found a fallen branch. Wading a few steps into the pond, she extended the branch to him and pulled him up on shore. He lay on his side in the moonlight, coughing and gasping for air.

McGrew, who had been watching the whole thing from the house, came rushing up. He bent over his nephew.

"John, my boy. Are you alright? Here, Maggie—Good God, girl, stop that laughing and help me get him on his feet." When they got him standing, John pitched forward and vomited into the weeds.

"Just swallowed some of the pond," McGrew said encouragingly. "Nothing to worry about, happens to the best of us. Now get on back to the house, my boy. Get into some dry clothes, you'll catch a chill out here."

John nodded dumbly and started for the house, coughing and shaking himself like a wet dog.

McGrew stood quietly, the tips of his fingers arched together.

"Maggie," he said at last, "sit down. We need to have a talk."

Maggie looked away. "Too mad to sit." she said.

"Very well. Stand, then. We'll talk anyway. I gather . . ." here McGrew took a moment in choosing his words. "I gather John's proposal didn't set well with you."

Maggie turned to the older man, scarcely able to believe her ears. "You mean you knew about this fool idea?"

McGrew cleared his throat. "Well, surely. This is a family matter, of course. John and I discussed this at great length before he came to you.

"Maggie, I will ask you to indulge me for a few moments more. You see, there are a number of advantages to this marriage, advantages which will benefit us all. If John listens to me, he will be a rich and influential man someday. The name of McGrew will be as good as gold in this region.

"All my holdings will go to him—and you, if you be his wife. I've always thought of you as a daughter and I see no reason why we shouldn't make it official in the eyes of God, if you know what I mean."

"I don't think God had much to do with this," Maggie said.

"Ah, now, child. That is where you are wrong. It is almost as though all this was pre-ordained. All the pieces fit so perfectly. Take your bread-baking business, for instance."

"It's not a business," Maggie interrupted, "it's a calling."

"Now that is where you are wrong. It is a business, and a very fine one at that. Although it could be a much better one if it were managed properly.

"With your bread-baking operation located here on the premises, it would be a tidy addition to the millwork we already do. John and I would handle the marketing of your work and all you would have to do is concern yourself with the baking you do so well. No need to worry yourself about the business end of things."

"It's not a business," Maggie repeated.

"Well, I won't dwell on this subject any longer. Think on it. But I'll warn you: I wouldn't take too long in making up my mind. I dare say, John is probably the most eligible bachelor in the valley and another girl just may catch his eye. After all, a girl on the frontier doesn't have many chances at marriage. She'd be wise to make the best of her circumstances. Will you think about what I've said, Maggie?"

She said nothing.

"Well, then, I'll be saying goodnight. You think on what I've said." Then he was gone.

Maggie reached down for her packbasket. "Foolish talk," she muttered, not sure who she was talking to.

The next morning, John officially began his courtship of Maggie Callahan. He showed up at the cabin just after breakfast, pulling along a mule, loaded with flour barrels from the mill.

"Good morning," he sang out when Maggie came to the doorway, "Uncle Joseph said it's time we bring you another load of flour. Where do you want it?"

Maggie heaved a deep breath. "Bring it inside, John."

John got the barrels stowed away safely in the corner and dusted off his hands.

"You sure do need a man around here," he was saying. "Why, there's many a chore around here either too hard or dangerous for a woman to do. I have a little time before I need to be back. Is there any little thing I can do for you around here?"

Maggie thought she might give him something simple to keep him out of her hair.

"There's a woodpile out behind the house," she said, "You could split up some kindling for me."

John rolled up his sleeves and took her long-handled axe down from the shelf where it lay. He glanced once at the keen edge she had put on it then disappeared out the doorway.

Maggie turned back to the bread dough she had been kneading. A moment later she heard a piercing yell. She dashed out the doorway and around to the woodpile. John lay on the ground, his face as white as a sheet. The axe lay in the grass beside him. Blood was seeping from a clove in his boot where the axeblade had slashed through the leather and into his foot.

Maggie knelt down and eased the boot off his foot. "Lay back," Maggie instructed, "don't look at it, for God's sake." Even though the boot was filled with blood, Maggie could see that John still had all his toes.

"You just slashed your foot along the side, you fool," she said. John groaned.

"Oh, quit carryin' on like ya cut yer foot off," she said.

She used his sock to mop up most of the blood then stepped into the meadow and carefully lifted a spider's web up off an arching grass stem. She laid the filmy web over the cut.

"What are you doing?" John said in horror.

"Spider's web will help the blood clot up," Maggie answered, "it'll stop the bleeding real quick." She wrapped up the wound as she spoke.

"I have just a peck of things planned to do today," she went on, "you'll have to ride the mule down to the mill by yourself. Don't walk on that foot—it'll just start the bleeding up again."

She went and got the tethered mule and brought it over and got John situated on the animal's back. John looked awfully pale. He clung to the packsaddle, his teeth gritted in pain.

"Give my regards to the family," Maggie said. Then she slapped the mule on the rump and watched it plod off down the trail.

Maggie turned and picked up the bloody axe. She

noticed that the axe handle was split. She sighed. She would have to whittle a new one now. And with so much to do today.

She looked down the trail after John.

"You know, Maggie," she said to herself, "taking care of a man like that would be a full-time job just in itself." Then she went to wash his blood from her hands so she could get back to the baking.

When Maggie next went to the mill, she saw that John's foot was healing well although he still limped a little.

"Too bad about John's foot," Maggie said to Mrs. McGrew when they were alone, working together in the kitchen.

"I wouldn't worry about him," the older woman snorted, "he's milking that injury for all it's worth. He's gotten out of a week's work at the mill already."

"He's a caution, I'll say that."

"Chip off the old block," Mrs. McGrew said.

Maggie took a deep breath. "John asked me to move down off the mountain and take up here on this property as his wife."

"I know." Mrs. McGrew said.

"Well, what do you say about it?"

"Marriage is one of the necessities of life, Maggie. It's a woman's entrance fee to adult life. Sometimes it's a high price to pay, but I don't know another way to do it." Then Mrs. McGrew shook her head. "No listen, Maggie, I don't want to make it sound all bad. Life is too hard to go it alone. Don't pull a single harness all your life, that's what I say. It may not seem on the outside that Joseph and I have an ideal marriage, but it works well enough.

"As far as I can tell, when it comes to marriage, men are pretty much the same—they are all equally unsatisfactory. But since marriage is what we must do, seems to me the trick is to pick the one who is the best provider and who has the good sense to leave you the run of the house and leave you be the balance of your waking hours."

Mrs. McGrew wagged a finger at Maggie. "Establish your territory and defend it. Oh, you can give them the trappings of power, the looks of it. But, you know, Maggie, the real power in the community is the power of the family, and that is in the woman's domain. Without the women to hold the family together, none of the sweating, and grunting these men do would mean anything. Remember that Maggie, and you'll have a better marriage than most. That's all I'll say to you Maggie, knowing that you'll do what you will anyway."

The older woman's words had a chilling effect on Maggie. She felt as though she were offering herself up as some great sacrifice for some unknown cause. When she returned to the cabin that night, her feet naturally guided her up the deer trail, to the mountain top where she had stood so many times.

She looked out across the peaceful valley then turned her gaze, as she always did, to the west. And, like always, her thoughts turned to Franny. "What would Franny say about all this?" Maggie asked herself. Then, an instant later, she knew. Her heart reached for Franny out across the wilderness miles and she wished her aunt was back in the valley. But she knew what she would say: "Look past your nose, Maggie, and don't be afraid of nothin'."

"Now what does that mean?" Maggie thought. "Does it mean don't be afraid to take the leap into marriage? Or does it mean don't be afraid to make your own way, husband or not?"

Looking out across the dark mountain ridges, the answer came to her.

"No," she said to herself. "I won't do it. As long as I have a place of my own and can stand on my own two feet, I won't give myself up to a man I don't want, even if his name is McGrew."

She turned and went down the mountainside and climbed into bed, feeling settled and resolute. Maggie had no way of knowing this would be the last night she would spend in the cabin she loved so well.

Chapter Eleven

John's foot healed. Urged on by his matrimonial aspirations, he resumed his courting of Maggie.

In the afternoon, while they were alone in the cabin, John laid a hand on Maggie's shoulder.

Her voice took on a hard edge. "John," she said, "I don't have a millpond to pitch you in up here but I won't hesitate to bark your shins if you lay a hand on me again."

John drew his hand back and responded with his usual good humor. "You'll come around to it, Maggie. All the women do eventually."

Then he changed the subject. "What can I do for you today? Just must be a mess of things that need done around here with me laid up for so long."

"Only women's work," Maggie said. "I'm boiling up

clothes and blankets and washrags today."

"I'll lend a hand just the same," John said.

Maggie sighed. She had known mosquitos like this man. They were troublesome, but hardly worth bothering about.

"Oh, alright," she said, "get that big kettle and bring it out into the meadow. There's a hangin' tripod out there. I'll carry some of this fire out and get the wood started."

Maggie got the fire going before she realized that she was out of soft soap.

She put her hands on her hips.

"Now, we'll just have to haul all this gear back in and do it some other day," she said.

John glanced at the sun. "Plenty of daylight left," he said, "I'm sure Aunt Maura has some she can loan you. Why don't I stay here and watch this fire for you and you can go down and fetch back that soap."

"Well," Maggie agreed, "that would be a help. Alright. Keep an eye on that fire, though. It's awful windy today and the fire could get away from ya if ya don't pay attention. I'll be back in an hour with that soap."

Maggie tied on her bonnet and left.

As soon as she was out of sight, John found himself a comfortable place in the shade. The late afternoon sun was warm and full on the meadow. The smells of the crab apple blossoms filled the air. John laid back, his hands behind his head.

The wind rifted through the tree branches overhead, dislodging blossoms which rained down and fell all around him. "Nothing like being in love," he told himself. Then he closed his eyes and let the drowsiness of the afternoon take him.

When he woke, his first sensation was one of intense heat. He opened his eyes and they were instantly stung by thick smoke. Coughing, he sat up and looked around him.

The worst had happened. The wind had scattered the fire out across the dead leaves and the whole clearing was afire!

The leafy groundcover had caught first, then the tall grass. A few dead pines, still standing, had begun to burn with a menacing crackling sound.

John could see that the cabin was still untouched but that the wind was rapidly pushing the ever-widening ring of fire in that direction. A moment later, obeying his most primal instincts, John found himself running downhill, away from the flames.

Maggie heard him before she saw him. He came crashing down the trail, sounding like a herd of stampeded woods buffalo. Then Maggie saw him, racing headlong down the trail, hollering in a voice scorched raw with heat and fear. She couldn't understand a word he was saying.

"What is it?" she shouted.

John collapsed against a tree trunk beside her.

"Fire!" was all he could manage. "It's afire!"

Maggie looked up the mountainside and saw a billow of smoke rising above the treetops.

"Oh no!" she said. "Come on, ya got to go back up there with me!"

John shook his head. "Can't. It's too much for the two of us. We gotta go to the mill for help."

Maggie grabbed him by the front of his shirt and shook him.

"No time for that. The whole mountainside'll be gone by then," she shouted.

She didn't wait for an answer. She began dragging him up the mountainside with her. At some point he began running along on his own. They topped the shoulder of the mountain together and dashed up onto the flat.

When Maggie saw the clearing ablaze she couldn't help but exclaim, "Good God! It's afire!"

And it was. The underbrush had been burnt black for a hundred feet on the upwind side of the washing fire. But it hadn't reached the cabin yet.

"There's nothing we can do," John shouted, "even if we had enough buckets, we could never carry enough water from the stream—"

"No!" Maggie said, her eyes ablaze, "you don't fight a

fire like this with buckets. There was one like this last year down at General Potter's. He had the men get shovels and rakes and clear a fire lane—it looked kinda like a long wide road where all the burnable things were swept back out of the way. That way the fire will stop along that line and burn itself out.

"Understand? We can do the same thing here." Maggie reached down and picked up two sturdy branches laying at her feet. "We can use these. Are you with me?"

John nodded. "Alright. Where do we start?"

Maggie glanced around. "Look how the wind's blowin', carryin' that fire towards the cabin. I figure we can let it burn over there on the eastern side of the clearing—the stream's over there and it'll just get to the stream and burn itself out. I think what we got to do is scrape ourselves a path clean across the clearing in between the fire and the cabin. We can start here and take it all the way over to the banks of the stream."

"Just rake back the leaves and brush, right?" John asked.

"Sure, anything that burns. Let's get moving! I'll start here, you begin over at the stream, we'll work our way in and meet in the middle."

John nodded and dashed across the clearing, keeping ahead of the flames.

Maggie moved as fast as she could go, clearing herself a path. She had to run ahead of the flames, working in the intense heat and smoke, coughing and wiping her eyes to see.

She worked furiously, her breath came in choking sobs. The wind gusted, blowing the flames right up to where she worked. Then she saw John, his long arms flying, working up close to her. They were almost there! They had made it! The path was almost complete. The heat was nearly unbearable by now. Some of the flames caught on the edge of Maggie's billowing skirt. She tried to beat them out with her hands but the wind just gusted them higher. Suddenly she was surrounded by flames. She was on fire! Seized by a terrible panic, she dropped her stick and began running across the clearing, thinking she could outrun the flames. But her running just fanned the flames higher.

John saw what was happening. He acted instantly. It took him a few moments to catch her because she was running so fast. He tackled her and rolled her on the ground, smacking out the flames with his hands. He tore off his shirt and used it to smother the flames on her dress.

Maggie lay dazed in the dirt, her dress still smoking.

"Maggie?" John's voice was urgent.

She rose up on an elbow. "I'm alright. Where's the fire

now?" She shielded her eyes with her hands and looked. The fire to the east was burning fiercely towards the stream. She knew she'd just have to let that end of the clearing go. But the fire headed toward the cabin had stopped. Her idea had worked!

"We did it!" Maggie shouted. "We stopped the fire!" she put her arms around John's neck and hugged him.

"Lay back now, Maggie, you should see how badly burnt you are. You stay right here. I'll get down to the mill just as fast as I can and get help up here. You lay quiet," John said.

He got to his feet and dashed off across the smoking field, running in smooth, long-legged strides.

Maggie lay her face down on the charred earth. She looked down at her body then forced herself to look away when she saw the blackened skin and places where the clothing stuck to her flesh. But the cabin was safe. That was the most important thing.

Then an incredible thing happened. The wind gusted strong across the clearing and the fire, like an advancing army, jumped the fire lane and roared to life in the tall grass around the cabin!

Somehow, Maggie managed to pull herself to her feet. She had no choice now. She was alone. And she knew she was going to have to build another fire lane now, closer in to the cabin, like a moat around a castle.

She stumbled through the smoke and flames and found herself a branch to use as a tool. Then she began the exhausting, frenetic work of clearing a new fire path. She would make this one wider, she told herself, wide so that no wind-blown flames could jump it.

She worked furiously. But she was not fast enough. The woodpile caught first. The thin kindling she had split and stacked went up like a matchbox.

Then the hemlock-bark roof caught. Maggie tried to beat the flames back but it was no use. She was surrounded on all sides by fire, backed up against the log wall. Her hair and clothing began to catch. She knew then that she couldn't save Franny's cabin. It would be all she could do to save herself.

Maggie bent low and leaped through a wall of flame, running on sheer instinct, slapping out her burning clothes as she ran.

She stumbled out across the desolate burnt-over ground until she came to the stream. She fell headlong into the shallow water and lay there, rolling in the wet mud. She soaked her dress in water and used it to cover her eyes and mouth and nose so she could breathe the hot smoky air. Trees overhead burnt and dropped flaming branches down in the water all around her. She lay there for hours, listening to the mountainside burn. Somewhere in the middle of the heat and the smoke and the flames, she lost consciousness.

It was just before dark when John lead the McGrews and a group of neighbors up to the site of the fire. The men stumbled around in the poor light, calling Maggie's name. There was no answer.

"We gotta find her," he begged.

John was astonished to see that the cabin had burnt. The marks on the ground told the story.

"I left her right over there," John said, pointing.

"Easy, boy," McGrew said. Then, when the young man was out of earshot, McGrew said to one of the other men, "I just hope to God Maggie didn't go back into the cabin."

They knew there was nothing to be done in the dark. Coaxing John away, the party left and headed back down to the mill, resolved to continue the search at first light.

It was the light that woke Maggie. That and the chill from laying in the streambed all night. Summoning up all of her strength, Maggie dug her fingers into the mud and pulled herself up onto the bank.

In the eerie pre-dawn light, the clearing looked like the scene of a terrible battle. Smoke still hung in the air. Here and there, small fires were still smouldering. Everywhere, there was the blackened, charred ugliness the fire had left behind.

Then Maggie's eyes fell on the cabin and a cry escaped from her heat-cracked lips.

Nothing stood but a framework of charred timbers and Franny's stone chimney, towering above the smoking ruins.

Dazed, Maggie rose to her knees, then her feet, and walked across the clearing. She stepped through the charred doorway and into the ruins of the cabin. The floor was knee-deep in ash and the blackened timbers slanted dangerously down into the rubble.

Maggie's knees gave way under her and she found herself kneeling down by the fireplace hearth. She began to rummage aimlessly through the ashes. Her hand struck something hard. She pulled it out. It was the broken paddle of Franny's bread-baking peel. She sat in the rubble, the broken peel blade cradled in her lap, and looked up at the chimney towering over her.

"Well," she said in a cracked voice, "I always wanted a summer kitchen. Now I have one." She laughed. But the laugh got choked off halfway through and turned into an anguished cry. She bent her head and sobbed. Her teardrops dropped into the ashes. She knew this was the end of something.

When the men came into the clearing they found her

sitting just that way in the ashes. They made a stretcher from a blanket and gently carried her down to the mill and put her to bed.

It was two days before she could talk. All the while John sat faithful by her bedside, helping Mrs. McGrew and Annie with the cold compresses and fetching water by the dipper for Maggie's parched throat.

McGrew came in to see her when she seemed lucid.

"A tragedy, no other way to say it," he remarked. "You're fortunate to be alive."

Maggie nodded. "Yes," was all she said.

"But tell me, child, how did the blaze start? John will say nothing about it. It's a mystery to me."

Maggie looked over and saw John sitting nearby. His eyes searched for hers, as though he were pleading her to keep the terrible secret. She felt a sudden, almost overpowering rage toward him and she was about to speak up, tell them all what a careless fool he had been and how it had all been his fault.

Then she looked down and caught a glimpse of his swelled and bandaged hands. And she remembered that he had saved her life by beating out the flames on her body with his bare hands. In a strange way, her heart went out to him.

She saw that McGrew and his wife were waiting for an

answer.

"Oh, it was just the wind, you know," she said. "I had a washing fire going outside and the wind just took it. Nothing anybody could have done about it. We did all we could."

John breathed a sigh of relief and looked down at the floor between his feet.

A few days later, Maggie got a visitor. It was Jake Logan. When he came into the room, he was shocked at how pale and thin Maggie seemed but he didn't let it show in his face. He grinned big.

"Good to see ya girl," he said.

"It's all gone, Jake," she said, "All of it—Franny's cabin, the land, the garden."

The old man shook his head sadly.

"I seed it all, girl. And no point dwellin' on what's gone. The question is: What will you do now?"

Maggie laughed sadly. "Only two choices, way I see it. I could stay on here and be a bound-out girl again. I suppose they'd allow that. If the McGrew's wouldn't take me in, I suppose someone would. I thought about rebuilding the cabin but the ground's ruint for a few seasons and it's the busy time of year now, no way we could throw a cabin up there before the fall. So that leaves one other choice. Did you hear about the marriage?"

Jake nodded. "The Widda Brown fills me in on the gossip."

"Well, might be time I was married. Have a new house here on these grounds, have my own place again."

Jake nodded. "The signs seems to point that way. McGrews ain't such bad folks. Although that young fella—what's his name?"

"John."

"Yeah, John, he'd be a real challenge as a husband, now wouldn't he?"

"I'd be marrying the family, not the man," Maggie said.

Jake nodded. "I suppose."

Then Maggie brightened. "So what about you, Jake, just passing through or are you staying a while?"

"Think I'll stay some. Permanent, maybe."

Maggie perked up her ears.

"What do you mean?" she asked.

"Well, you know, a man gets to be my age he gets tired of haulin' his bones all over the mountains. I believe this winter was the coldest one I ever spent up north. Man gets to feel like he should have something to call his own, you know. So the Widda Brown, she's been talking about me taking up with her on her place down the creek. She's a good woman, in her own way. The signs seems to be pointing all in one direction for both of us girl. It's taking a mate, somewheres along the way, just another part of life, you know."

Maggie nodded.   "Maybe so, Jake."

After the old man left, Maggie felt very tired. She laid back and stared at the wooden beams overhead. John came in with a bucket of cool water.

"Wish that old man would stay clear of here," he said, "gives me the creeps, he does. I brung you some water, Mag."

Maggie lifted her head a little. "Thanks." He held her head while she drank. Then she laid back.

John sat in the chair and pulled it close to her bedside. "Maggie, you'll be up and around before long, and I think there's plans got to be made. I want to take care of you, Maggie, we all do. And I want us to set up a place here on this ground and raise kids. Alright, Maggie?"

Maggie lay silent.

"Alright?" he asked again.

Maggie closed her eyes. "Alright," she said. She sighed. She was very tired.

The news of the coming wedding spread like wildfire. And McGrew was sparing no expense to make it the most grandiose occasion the valley had ever seen. For him, it was more than just the marriage of a nephew. To McGrew, it symbolized a new elevation in the wilderness empire he planned to build under the name of McGrew.

McGrew's enthusiasm was infectious. All the month of May and right up until the June wedding, folks in the valley cooked and sewed and readied themselves for the occasion. McGrew had arranged for a circuit-riding preacher to come into the valley especially for the ceremony. The women had set up an area outdoors, down by the millpond, for a proper wedding ceremony.

The morning of the wedding, Maggie put on her extra dress and Annie took her down to the pond to fix her hair.

Maggie's burns had healed well now. She felt her strength returning. She felt as though her body was tingling all over.

"Maggie McGrew . . . Maggie McGrew," she said to herself. She kept saying it over and over. It sounded to her like she was talking about someone else.

Before Annie brushed out her hair, she sat Maggie by the water and began signing to her.

"I've got a wedding present for you here. Open it now so I can see your face. I wanted it to be special." Annie laid a small package, wrapped in canvas, on the ground between them. Maggie unwrapped it and looked at the treasured gift. She held it up in the morning light. It was a deerskin pouch, like the one she carried the spook yeast in.

"Your old one looked pretty worn," Annie signed, "so I

thought you might want to start your new life with a new pouch."

Maggie smiled. "It means a lot. Thanks, little squirrel."

Just then the girls saw someone emerge from the trees on the other side of the pond. It was Jake. He came around to their side of the water quickly.

He made the greeting sign to Annie and nodded to Maggie. He was dressed in full buckskins, complete with hunting pouch and rifle.

"You look like you're goin' huntin' today, Jake," Maggie said.

"That I am girl."

"Thought you came to see me get married off."

"Can't stay for that," he shook his head. "Gotta move."

Maggie shook her head. "What do you mean?"

"What I'm saying' girl, is I'm afraid this is goodbye."

"But why?"

"Had a long talk last night with the Widda Brown. She figured that preacher only comes through every now and then and that if he was gonna be here we oughta take this chance to get ourselves married in the eyes of God and all. And Maggie, the thing that scares me about it is that I want to do it.

"But, girl, I knowed in my heart of hearts these bones still got some ramblin' left in 'em and I'm gonna light on outa here before I ferget that. The Widda Brown's a good woman, but I don't know that I'd make a good husband. So I'm headed out west now. Sorry I can't stay for the weddin'. Jest wanted to come by to say my goodbyes."

"But where will you be?" Maggie asked.

Jake nodded westward. "Somewheres out there, beyond them mountain ranges."

"That's where Franny is," Maggie said. The words came out of her mouth before she could stop them.

"Wal, yes it is," Jake said.

"Jake, if you see her—tell her about me, will you?"

"Surely, girl, but I don't think the chances is too great—"

"Good God," Maggie exclaimed, "I wish I was goin' with you."

"Now, girl you don't mean that. This marriage thing may not be all that bad fer young girl like you. Now you take an idee into your head like this, it could ruin a young girl's life."

"I know it, I know it," she said, "but it just doesn't set right with me. Besides, I'm too young to get married."

Jake laughed. "So am I."

"Well, then: Will you take me with you—West and to find Franny?"

Jake smiled. "Girl, yer makin a serious mistake."

Maggie smiled back, "So are you."

"Well, then," the old man said, "let's make 'er together. Franny will tan my hide when we find her and tell her about this."

Maggie laughed. "I think Franny'd do the same were she in my shoes."

Jake nodded. "Yeah, girl, I s'pose she would. Well, we better scurry on outa here before they realize the bride is missin'."

Maggie turned to Annie. The younger girl had been following the lip-talk and was smiling too.

"Here, Annie. I want to give you something." She pulled her old pouch from inside her dress and pinched out half of the spook yeast, put it in the new pouch and hung it around Annie's neck.

"You keep the bread bakin' alive in this valley now, won't ya?"

Annie nodded, the tears coming up in her eyes.

Maggie smiled. "You know the bread baking secrets, Annie, and you're The Bread Sister now."

The girls embraced for a long moment there by the millpond. Maggie thought about the first day she had met the girl, two years before.

"She will be a good Bread Sister to this valley," Maggie thought, "she has the heart for it."

"Now Annie, you'll have to stall them a little, give us time to get up over the mountain. Tell them I went up towards the cabin for something. That way they'll figure I just ran off and you won't be to blame, understand?"

Annie nodded. "Godspeed to you Maggie. You, too, Jake." She made the signs with her quick hands.

"No matter what, don't tell them where I went," Maggie said.

Annie shook her head and began signing. "I won't say a word." She smiled big.

Jake took Maggie by the arm, "Let's move now, I think some folks are coming down this way." They ducked into the trees and were gone.

They climbed fast up the trail for a ways until they came to a place where they could stand and look out over the valley. Down below, they could see wagons, horseback riders, folks from all over, converging on the mill ground.

Maggie could pick out the preacher in his dark coat and she could see John strutting, proud as a peacock, as people began to form up for the ceremony. And above it all, carrying up from the depths of the valley, she could hear McGrew's voice, rising theatrically above the crowd.

"Gather 'round, friends, gather 'round," he was saying, "and you will witness one of the most unforgettable spectacles this community has ever seen . . ."

Maggie turned to Jake, "You can say that again," she said. Then they laughed, their hearts light as birds, and turned up the mountain trail, headed west, toward Franny and the wild westward country.

The End

If you enjoyed this book . . .

You might be interested to know that Robin is now working on a second volume in the "Bread Sister" series. If you'd like to be placed on a mailing list to receive information when the second volume is ready, simply drop a line to Groundhog Press, P.O. Box 93, Wyncote, Pa. 19095.

About The Bread

The bread that Maggie Callahan and countless other frontier women baked was something we've come to call sourdough. Sourdough bread gets its name from the pungent yeasty smell given off by a well-aged sourdough starter, or "spook yeast" as Franny would call it.

Sourdough bread has a long and glorious history, dating back to ancient times. But this bread really came into its own on the American frontier. Pioneering families, far from the comforts of their homeland, wanted to bring along the goodness of home-baked bread.

But why was it that sourdough bread, in particular, became the choice of the frontier cook?

Besides the fact that there are few things on earth which can equal the downright delectability of sourdough bread, hot and fragrant from the oven, there are some practical reasons.

In order to make truly good bread, some form of leavening or rising is necessary. Leavened bread is generally more tasty and rides easier in the stomach.

Today we rise most of our breads with dry packaged yeast, a modern-day version of the ancient sourdough. But in Maggie's day packaged yeast simply hadn't been invented yet.

One method available was baking soda or "sody saleratus." But many cooks frowned on its use because folk belief had it that baking soda was harmful, causing sterility to those who chose to imbibe. Today we know this isn't true but it was a folk notion nonetheless. A further drawback of baking powder was that it wasn't always available in the remote wilderness communities we're talking about.

This left sourdough, or "spook yeast," as the most logical choice. It was simply made. All a frontier cook needed was flour and water to whip up a sourdough starter. Sourdough was transportable, storable, durable and cheap—tailor-made for the American frontier.

What is sourdough, really? Nothing more than flour and water allowed to ferment in a warm place. Yeast spores from the air collect and begin to thrive in the water-flour mixture, converting the starch in the flour into sugar. The resulting fermentation creates a buildup of gases which puff the loaf up to twice its size.

You can carry on the legacy of the Bread Sister today by baking your own sourdough bread at home.

My wife, Jacque, a magnificent sourdough cook in her own right, has tested and developed the following recipes, adapting them to modern-day kitchens.

Strangely enough, sourdough bakery starts with something called a starter. This is the "sponge" or "spook yeast" that Maggie carried around her neck. It is from this "starter" that all sourdough loaves are born.

The "Starter"

To make the starter, place one cup of milk in a non-metal container (a glass jar, a plastic bowl or a ceramic crock works fine). Allow milk to stand at room temperature for 24 hours. Stir in 1 cup flour. White, unbleached flour is a good choice. Leave uncovered in a warm place (80 degrees is ideal) for two to five days depending on how long it takes to begin souring and bubbling. A good place is near the pilot light of a gas stove.

Anywhere between 70-90 degrees is good. Chilly temperatures slow down the growth of the yeast while too much heat (over 110 degrees) kills the yeasties outright. If the starter starts to dry out, stir in some tepid water. Once it has a good, sour smell and is full of bubbles it is ready to use.

Always keep about 1-1/2 cups of starter on hand. Each time you use a portion of the starter, replenish it with equal amounts of milk and flour. Cover and store in the refrigerator. It's best if you use the spook yeast at least once a week. If you don't plan to use it for two or three weeks, it's a good idea to spoon out about half, discard it, then replenish what remains with flour and milk. If you don't plan to do any baking for several weeks, you can freeze it. Since the low temperature slows down the growth of the yeasties, allow it to stand at room temperature for 24 hours before using again.

Recipes

Now you're ready to begin baking. Here's a simple basic recipe, adapted for modern kitchens:

Ingredients:

1 cup sourdough starter

6 cups all-purpose unsifted flour

1 package dehydrated yeast

1 teaspoon sugar or honey

1 teaspoon salt

1/2 teaspoon baking soda

1 egg for glazing (optional)

Begin with all ingredients at room temperature. In a non-metal bowl, mix 1 package of yeast and 1/2 cup of lukewarm water. Stir in sugar until dissolved. Set aside for 10 minutes or until yeast becomes foamy.

Sift flour. Add 4 cups, leaving 2 cups to be added later on. Stir in salt and baking soda. Mix with a non-metal spoon. Turn the resulting dough into a large oiled bowl, cover with a damp towel and let rise until double, about 2 hours.

Add 1 cup flour to the risen dough. Use the remaining cup to flour the kneading board. Knead well. The dough should feel elastic and satiny. Knead for about 10 minutes, until the dough can no longer absorb more flour.

Shape the loaves by forming the dough into round, plump circles. You can make one large loaf or two smaller ones. Set aside on a greased cookie sheet for the second rising. Rise for two hours or until the dough doubles in size. Keep covered with damp towel.

When the second rising is completed, use a sharp knife to score a cross on the top of each loaf. Decide which type of crust you'd prefer: Tender or crusty. For tender crusts, brush the surface of the loaves with a beaten egg or oil. For crusty bread, place a pan filled with water in the oven or simply brush the surface with water.

Bake at 375 degrees. For two loaves, bake for 50

minutes. For one, bake between 60-70 minutes.

The loaves are done when they turn a medium brown and give off a hollow sound when tapped on the underside.

Enjoy!

Once you've mastered this recipe, you might want to try a more traditional, and more difficult one, similar to the kind Maggie and Franny might have followed. Note: This recipe requires about 18 hours.

Ingredients:

1 cup starter

6 cups all-purpose unsifted flour

2 teaspoons sugar, honey or molasses

1 pinch baking soda (if available)

2 teaspoons salt

1-1/2 cups warm water

Begin with all ingredients at room temperature. In a non-metal bowl, combine starter, flour and water, sugar and salt. Mix with a non-metal spoon and set aside uncovered, for 12 hours.

After first rising, add 1 cup flour and use the remaining cup to flour the kneading board. Add baking soda and knead well. Form into loaves and let rise on a greased cookie sheet for 4 hours.

When second rising is completed, prepare the loaves for

the oven and bake them in the same fashion as the first recipe.

This recipe requires more work but you'll be rewarded with a finer bread. Enjoy it, you earned it!

Once you've become an old hand at these bread recipes it will be a simple matter to start turning out biscuits, flapjacks, doughnuts and cakes—all from your own perkin' sourdough pot.

Besides the edible results, there are more exotic uses for sourdough. They say some Alaskan prospectors used to allow the starter to ferment enough to pour off a fiery alcoholic liquid called "hootch." I tried it one time and all I can say is you'd have to spend a pretty long winter alone and be pretty downright desperate to drink that stuff. But, as a wise man once said, necessity is the mother of invention.

Folklore also provides us with other uses for sourdough—as a bacteria-fighting medicine, some take a spoonful of the raw starter by mouth. Others used the remarkable stuff to chink the spaces between the logs in their cabins or plug up holes in their shoes.

Shoe repairs aside, sourdough is great stuff. After you've tasted the joys of sourdough cookery, and after your kitchen has been filled with the heavenly smells of fresh-baked bread, you'll understand why Jake would say: "Bread ain't bread lest it's rised up light and airy. Makes a man's mouth glad to chomp inta!"

About The Author

The Central Pennsylvania wilderness is a familiar place to me. I grew up there, in the great Nittany Valley, in the shadow of Tussey Mountain, in the historic village of Boalsburg.

I spent my boyhood tramping the forests and canoeing the rivers of Central Pennsylvania. I come from a long line of woodsmen. My father and my grandfather before me were good hunters and storytellers.

I left home at 18 and spent three years in the U.S. Army as an infantryman. I served for nine months as a combat soldier in the Republic of Vietnam with the 101st Airborne Division and the 173rd Airborne Brigade.

Back home, I went to college on the G.I. Bill and received a B.A. in Journalism from The Pennsylvania

State University. I was also fortunate to travel extensively during this period, camping and hoboing across North America, Europe, Canada and Mexico.

After graduating, I entered my "Henry David Thoreau" period. I moved into a cabin on First Mountain in Penns Valley and lived there for two and a half years—three winters and two summers. This is the spot where Franny's fictional cabin stands, near the present-day town of Potters Mills.

My wife, Jacque, picked me up hitchhiking one day. A year later we moved to Philadelphia.

Here the plot thickens. We went through a very frustrating period of adjustment to civilized life. Jacque began a successful career in healthcare administration. I tried several jobs, first in social work, then in journalism. I was eventually named managing editor of a national trade publication. Our son, Jesse, was born.

But the 9-to-5 life lacked the vitality of life in the mountains or on the road. I remembered the words of the famous hobo, Fryin' Pan Jack: "I never want to make the erroneous assumption that I can loan someone else my mind for eight hours a day and they'll return it to me in an unmutilated fashion." I began to look for alternatives.

My search took me back to my boyhood loves of woodcraft and storytelling. I began looking into the possibilities of telling stories and teaching woodcraft as a way of life.

A year later, I left my job to begin storytelling full-time. Three years later I am one of perhaps a hundred people in the country who make their living by telling stories. Most of my work is in schools, museums and libraries where I combine North American folktales with demonstrations of old-time living skills, aimed at fostering an appreciation for the natural world and a respect for the plants and animals who share the planet with us.

All in all, a guy would have to be crazy to complain about my life: I've got two great kids in Jesse and Rachel, a wife who's a real pioneer woman and a nice wooded spot of ground in Montgomery County, north of Philadelphia. Besides storytelling, I've been able to get involved in a lot of interesting writing, recording, teaching and craft projects which allow me to pursue what I do as an art form. In 1984 I formed Groundhog Press to put out a series of writing projects of which "The Bread Sister," is the first.

Basically, it all comes under the same heading: Live the dream.

About the Illustrator

William Sauts Bock has illustrated over 70 books during the past quarter century and has been honored by the *American Institute of Graphic Arts (A.I.G.A.),* New York. He is a member of the *Philadelphia Children's Reading Round Table,* and an educator on Art, Books, and his Native American (Lenape Indian) culture.

His books include such seemingly diverse subjects as: *Crusader King, Richard the Lionhearted; Sam Adams; Tom Sawyer; The Jersey Devil; Pirates;* and *Lincoln;* as well as full color sound/film productions about Lenape culture, *Robinson Crusoe, American Literature,* ancient *Greek* culture, and much more.

A graduate of the Philadelphia College of Art, he is also a Lutheran minister and served as a missionary to the Navaho Indians in Arizona. He is a lecturer in American Indian ethno-history and has traveled up and down the Susquehanna River by canoe to seek out important Indian sites. He is the friend of many American Indians and has been adopted into the Cherokee-Lenapes of Oklahoma who have given him the name of Netamuxwe.

Bock lives with his family in Souderton, Pennsylvania.

ORDER FORM

To order additional copies of *The Bread Sister,* simply fill out this form and send with check (payable to Robin Moore) to: Groundhog Press, P.O. Box 93, Wyncote, PA 19095.

Please send the following copies of *The Bread Sister:*

Quantity	Edition	Price	Total
_____	Hardback	$10	_____
_____	Paperback	$7	_____
		Postage & Handling $2 on each book	_____
		Enclosed	_____

Quantity Discounts available, Write for Information.

NAME _____

ADDRESS _____

CITY _____

STATE _____ ZIP _____